Hostage/Murder in Memphis

Hostage/Murder in Memphis

Terrence Schultz

Library of Congress Control Number: 2011907235
ISBN: Hardcover   978-1-4628-6841-4
                 Softcover   978-1-4628-6840-7
                 Ebook   978-1-4628-6842-1

To order additional copies of this book, contact:
Xlibris Corporation
1-888-795-4274
www.Xlibris.com
Orders@Xlibris.com
92743

CONTENTS

Foreword 9
Prelude 11

Chapter 1-Prelude To Disaster 13
Chapter 2-Officer Duties And Pay 1983 17
Chapter 3-The Theft Of The Purse 23
Chapter 4-Report Taken 25
Chapter 5-Lindberg Sanders 26
Chapter 6-Coleman Calls Dispatch 31
Chapter 7-Dispatch Sends A Car To Shannon Street 35
Chapter 8-The Assault Begins 38
Chapter 9-Hester Profile 42
Chapter 10-Hester Taken Hostage 47
Chapter 11-Help Arrives 48
Chapter 12-Tommy Turner 50
Chapter 13-Russ Aiken 53
Chapter 14-Reserve Officers 58
Chapter 15-Heroes 67
Chapter 16-Ed Vidulich 69
Chapter 17-St. Jude Children's Hospital 71
Chapter 18-Rescue At St. Jude 73
Chapter 19-Negotiations With Sanders 75
Chapter 20-Family Brought In 78
Chapter 21-No Demands 80
Chapter 22-Listening Devices 82
Chapter 23-The Thin Blue Line 85
Chapter 24-Hours Drag On 87

Chapter 25-Decision Time 89
Chapter 26-Assault Preparations 93
Chapter 27-The Rescue Begins 96
Chapter 28-Aftermath 105

Ramifications 109
Epilogue 133
Where Are They Now? 139
Index 145

Dedication

My deepest gratitude goes out to my family and especially my lovely wife without whose support, encouragement, and love made this endeavor possible. She has been a ray of sunshine in my darkest hours and I could never thank her enough, or put into words everything that she means to me. Thank you, Brenda.

I spoke with many different people in compiling the data for this book. I want to specifically thank Jim Kellum who provided insights I would have never imagined. He is quite a guy . . .

Russ Aiken was friendly, hospitable, humble, and one hell of a man. He is one of the most impressive individuals I have ever met. Enjoy your retirement. You deserve it.

Jim Smith provided leads and proved invaluable in finding resources after some twenty-five years.

All of the staff in the records department at 201 could not have been more supportive and helpful.

"Fat" Sanders offered prospective from the family's side of the tragic events that fateful night in Memphis. He is truly a class act and even though he and his entire family suffered horribly, he still retains a sense of humor and dignity that his father would be proud of.

Lastly, I want to offer my heartfelt appreciation to a couple of retired Memphis Officers who were invaluable to me in my research. They did not wish to be named in the book and I respect their wishes. I want them both to know that without their help this book would never have been written. Thanks guys.

FOREWORD

I graduated from college in 1974 with an active interest in law enforcement. I had applied for a position, while still in college, with the Chicago Police Department and eventually was hired. The hiring process with the Chicago Police can take years. In the interim, I had gotten married, bought my first house, and had secured a job with a company that was paying me $1,200 per month. The Chicago Police at that time was paying only $750 a month, so my choice was made. I continued working and eventually became an officer with the police department in the city (Chicago) I grew up in. I worked for that department for five years before relocating to Simi Valley, California. However, I never lost the desire to return to work in law enforcement again. I followed news stories about policing religiously. In 1983, I heard about a story in Memphis, Tennessee, where a police officer and his partner were on a routine call and tragedy struck. Both officers were taken hostage and one escaped, although seriously wounded having been shot twice and beaten severely, but his partner was held for over thirty hours and systematically tortured and beaten during this time. The police were trying to negotiate to secure his freedom during this time, but ultimately, they were forced to make entry into the house where the officer was being held, and seven people ended up dead along with the officer taken hostage. That story remained in the back of my mind for many years.

As fate would have it, I was transferred to Memphis in 1990, and I made my home in one of the suburbs. My son inherited my interest in law enforcement and was hired as a full-time police officer in 2007. I joined the reserve program in the same community in 2004 and had the opportunity to talk with a number of

9

people who were involved in the now-famous Shannon Street incident (although Shannon Avenue is more accurate in that it is officially an avenue, not a street).

This piqued my interest once again in this long forgotten footnote in Memphis police history. I quit my job in 2008 and began interviewing people formally who were there that fateful day in 1983 with the intention of telling the story of the tragedy at Shannon Avenue.

The more I investigated, the more the story took on a more meaningful purpose to me. The horror that was Shannon Avenue was a story that needed to be told. What began as a project to tell a story became a labor of love. I wondered, at the time of the occurrence, how a team of police officers could stand idly by while their brother officer was being held hostage and do nothing. I was determined to find out. What I found was that every officer there was a victim. The tragedy touched more lives than I could ever imagine. This is their story.

PRELUDE

Officer Ray Schwill lay bleeding from gunshot wounds to his hand and his head. He knew he was in deep trouble and that he had to escape somehow. He was pretending to be dead so that the thugs hovering over him would stop the torture. He was about to go into shock and knew it. If he did, he would not be able to control his breathing, and his tormentors would notice his chest heaving as he gulped in air. He had to control it somehow. Help was on the way so if he could only hold out a little longer. His partner was in horrible pain. Schwill could hear him screaming for help, but what could he do? If he could somehow create enough of a distraction, then he might just be able to escape out the front door, which was only a couple of feet away. He had just enough energy to make it; all he needed was the chance. Suddenly, gunfire erupted from the rear of the house. He heard footsteps running away from him in the direction of the shots. He stole a glance and noticed no one around him. There was one guy standing near the front window, but he was looking outside, not at him. He saw his chance and leaped toward the safety of the doorway. Would he make it in time?

Shannon Avenue

CHAPTER 1

Prelude to Disaster

On a bitter cold, dark January night in 1983, three Memphis police officers sat huddled around the little heat generated off the hood of one of their Dodge Diplomat patrol cars. They were talking about things cops usually talk about—the job, women, sports, etc. They had just finished coffee and decided to talk a few more minutes before going out on patrol. It was miserable out there this night, and no one was in any particular hurry to get started. Officer Bobby Hester had been entertaining the other cops with his outrageous stories and funny jokes. It was never dull with Bobby Hester around. He was always telling jokes and playing pranks on his fellow officers. He couldn't wait to get home and let his wife know what he had done to the victims of his jokes. His fellow cops didn't mind either. It was all in good fun, and you could not help but laugh at Bobby Hester.

Since the thugs and bad guys had to contend the same bitter conditions the cops did, they expected a slower-than-normal shift. Most bad guys didn't want to be in the cold anymore than the cops did. A hardy few might use the cold to commit crimes as they thought the cops would be hunkered down for the night, out of the cold. This was the furthest thing on the minds of the young officers this night. They didn't hang around long. It was just too cold to be out, and since the heaters in the cars were always cranked up to the max, relief was right behind the glass. Two of the officers were working together, and the third was going to be working with a new rookie officer.

His job was to bring this officer along and teach him the proper policing methods that worked best on the street. Not the spit-and-polish crap taught in the academy, but training that he might actually use one day. He took this responsibility seriously. It was not the first time Russ Aiken had been given the responsibility to train a new officer. John Wesley Sykes Jr. was the latest rookie to be teamed with Patrolman Aiken. He had worked with him only a short time, and he was progressing along quite nicely. He was taking to his training out on the streets well. He thought that one day he would become a fine officer for the Memphis Tennessee Police Department. New Year's Eve was fast approaching, and Aiken had decided to take the holiday off. Sykes was turning into a levelheaded, intelligent patrolman, and Aiken thought that having him teamed up with a different partner for New Year's Eve would be all right. Not much happened most New Year's Eve shifts, just a few drunks driving around, and that was about it. He had a wedding to attend, and it was important to his wife that they go together. He had plenty of vacation time available, so he put in to take that night off. On New Year's Eve of 1982, since his regular partner Officer Aiken was off duty, Sykes was scheduled to work with another officer, Patrolman Charlotte Creasy. Usually, when new officers hit the streets fresh out of the academy, departments would have them work with a number of different patrolmen.

This gave the new guys a more rounded, balanced experience to draw from. They could see how other officers handled situations and learned different tactics and methods to handle all the calls. During their shift, Creasy noticed a car driving erratically. It was driving too fast and weaving in and out of traffic. No doubt, just another New Year's Eve reveler who started a little early. They figured it was pretty routine.

The car was a beat-up old Pontiac with the muffler dragging along the ground. A real piece of crap. When Officer Creasy activated the overhead lights, they refused to stop for the officers. Like most pursuits police officers find themselves involved in, they had no idea why this car was refusing to stop. Many different emotions run through the minds of officers when a car refuses to stop over a minor traffic violation. Most are surprised initially, and then, they begin to get angry. Their authority is being questioned, and they don't like it. Their first response is to activate lights and siren and begin the pursuit. Then the adrenaline begins flowing, and the heart is pumping away, and it's off to the races. It was Sykes first high-speed pursuit, and the adrenaline was building. They chased the car for a few miles before they got it cornered in a darkened cove. The cops had the car right where they wanted it, trapped in a cove with only one way in or out—right where the officers' car was. As Creasy, who was driving the squad car, pulled into the cove, they were not exactly certain where the car was. It was very dark, and the cove offered little in the way of lighting. In fact, the car they were chasing had turned facing the officers and had extinguished their headlights. They watched the squad car ease into the cove. They waited a few seconds, and they suddenly turned on the lights, temporarily blinding the officers in pursuit. They accelerated quickly, aiming the car directly at the officers, who were now out of position and facing the opposite way. As they passed the squad car, two shots rang out from the suspect's vehicle.

Sykes, who was wearing his department issued bulletproof vest, heard the shots as they shattered the passenger-side window. One bullet creased the very top of his vest and then entered his neck. A fraction of an inch lower and the vest would have deflected the bullet, and Sykes would no doubt have a few sore ribs and a great story to tell his grandchildren. He died an hour and a half later at the hospital. When cars responding to the frantic cries for help arrived on the scene, they found Officer Creasy cradling Sykes's head in her lap as he bled profusely. Creasy was crying and pleading with him to wake up.

Creasy and Sykes had no way of knowing that the two subjects in the Pontiac had just committed an armed robbery at a local post office and were fleeing from the scene when they encountered the Memphis squad car. They had been under the assumption that they were simply chasing another drunk driver. After all, it was New Year's Eve.

The two armed robbers in the Pontiac had assumed that these officers were pursuing them because of the holdup at the post office. In reality, the call of an armed robbery had not even gone out yet from dispatch. In the twenty-first century, this probably would not have unfolded the way that it did. Police officers today involved in high-speed pursuits for minor traffic violations are almost immediately ordered to terminate the pursuit. It is not worth chasing someone over minor infractions if it puts the public in jeopardy. Also, liability concerns have forced most municipalities to order the cessation of all pursuits unless a violent felony has been committed. Crimes against property do not rate a pursuit. It is simply not worth the danger a pursuit poses to the public and the officers.

Officer Russ Aiken wonders to this day what would have happened had he not taken that night off. Guilt tugs at him, even though he has nothing to feel guilty about. What happened to Officer Sykes was a tragedy (Sykes had graduated from the academy only thirteen days earlier. He is the only probationary police officer in the history of the city of Memphis to be killed while on duty), and Aiken had no way of knowing what would happen that night. He knows this and yet still struggles with it. It is the type of man he is. A real cop's cop. He wasn't going to let this happen to any of the rookies he was given to train. No, sir, they were going to be taught properly, and it was his job to make this new officer the best street cop he could. That's the way things worked in the police department. You took care of your own. Once you put that uniform on, you became a member of a pretty exclusive fraternity. You looked out for your brother officer and he looked out for you. It simply was the way it worked. The men who shot Officer Sykes were caught shortly afterward. They were charged with the murder of a police officer along with many other crimes for their actions that night. Both were convicted.

As the three cops huddled around the squad car seeking warmth went their separate ways, no one could have imagined that destiny would bring them together this night once again, this time under horrendous conditions that would leave one of them brutally tortured to death, another scarred for life with multiple gunshot wounds, and another bearing witness to it all. All these men became heroes that tragic night, as did a number of others, and would suffer for years afterward, battling their own demons and suffering nightmares.

The call came in on January 13, 1983, and dispatch put the call out over the radio within minutes. Nothing seemed out of the ordinary. Just another report of a purse snatching on the mean streets of Memphis, Tennessee. Every officer goes on calls like this numerous times. Just another minor crime to investigate. Make the scene, take a report, and turn it over to the detectives to investigate and then on to the next call. Maybe the detectives would actually solve this crime, but neither officer really believed that was going to happen. Like all big cities in America, crime was running way ahead of the ability of the police department to stop it. There are some many much more violent crimes to solve: murders, rapes, assaults, robberies, etc. A simple purse snatching fell way low on the list of priorities for the detective division.

Earlier that day, a woman had been the victim of a random crime of opportunity all too common in Memphis. The incident occurred in a local grocery store, part of a large national chain of stores. Quitting time was approaching for a woman who worked at the store. While she was preparing to leave, she set her purse down and turned away. Something she had done hundreds of times in the past. However, this time, there was someone watching. With her attention diverted, someone simply grabbed her purse and walked away. When she went to leave, she was shocked to discover that her purse was gone. Some unknown, phantom person would play a pivotal role as the events of this day unfolded. He (or she) would never be identified or taken into custody. The tragedy that was set in motion with the simple theft of a purse would set the city of Memphis reeling. Whoever took this purse was probably looking to get a few extra bucks that day. Maybe they needed the money for drugs or liquor.

Junkies were a pretty common sight around that area. Little did this person realize that the act of stealing a purse would lead to the deaths of eight people. I doubt he is even aware of it today, some decades after the fact.

CHAPTER 2

Officer Duties and Pay 1983

In the 1980s, the pay for police officers in Memphis was barely enough to sustain a normal lifestyle. Every officer struggled to make ends meet at one time or another. Memphis was, and still is, one of the least expensive major metropolitan areas for people to reside in. Taxes are low, the state of Tennessee still has no state income tax, and utility rates are very reasonable, thanks to the Tennessee Valley Authority. Officers looked for every opportunity to earn a little extra money. Unlike firefighters whose schedule allowed them to work second jobs, policemen had no such luxury. They had to scramble to find second sources of income.

Overtime jobs helped bridge the gap between borderline poverty and a decent lifestyle. Most of the officers, at one time or another, worked overtime whenever and wherever it was available. The command staff knew that these overtime details were important to the rank and file and encouraged outside companies to hire off-duty officers as security. Most of the high-ranking officers in the department had worked these same jobs when they were on the streets, and they knew the extra money was welcome.

Conversely, the companies that hired off-duty police officers were happy to get them. They were commissioned law enforcement professionals who were better trained than private security guards. They performed their duties in their Memphis Police Department uniforms that the citizens all recognized. The cost was similar to what private security firms would charge, so why not hire real cops? And they are all armed and had radios with direct communication with dispatch.

Many other city employees, like firefighters, would sometimes earn more money in their second jobs than they did working for the city. Full-time firefighters usually worked at second jobs because they had so much free time. Police officers did not have the same free time that firefighters did. Firefighters would work forty-eight hours straight and then have seventy-two hours off. Police officers had to work a standard eight-hour shift, so the opportunity to work overtime was more restricted than it was for other municipal employees. These overtime details for officers were normally the best opportunity available for them to earn a few extra dollars. Many retail establishments used these officers consistently. Fast-food restaurants, drug stores, retail stores, all used officers periodically.

MPD History

The city of Memphis received its official charter in March 1827. One of the original founders of the city was the noted frontiersman Davy Crockett. In May of that same year, the first law enforcement official of the city was appointed as town constable similar to what is now commonly known as the chief of police. He has all the typical police powers, but the problem was that he was the only member of the fledgling department. The position was not even a full-time position at that time. Memphis had the reputation as a bawdy riverboat town. A single constable could do very little to stem the tide of criminal activity. And there was certainly plenty of that around in those days. Gambling, prostitution, gunfights were all too common sights in those early days. How much could one man do?

The second police constable was appointed a few years later. He had many of the same problems as his predecessor with murders becoming more of a problem than at any time in the past. To assist the new constable, the city council determined that the wharf master would also act with police powers primarily along the riverfront, and it was also decided that the constable would be entitled to half of whatever fines were collected for violations.

By 1839, the town had grown significantly. The city decided that more help was needed, so they hired two men to act as night watchmen. They were paid a few hundred dollars a year, and they alternated shifts each evening working from 10:00 p.m. until daylight. These watchmen actually had the authority to command ordinary citizens to assist them in times of need. If they refused, they were fined. It was decided that a building should be constructed to house the new employees, so the first police station was built in downtown Memphis for a few hundred dollars. The original employees did not carry guns. Instead, they were issued large clubs called rattlers. These rattlers could be used as clubs, but primarily, their use was intended as a means to alert ordinary citizens to their presence. It also had the side effect of warning the criminals as to their location. The noise made by these rattlers was created by the handle being connected to a ratcheting wheel. With a simple movement of the wrist, the loud noise was created. The night watchmen were also issued lanterns.

A few years later saw the first major confrontation between law enforcement and criminals. Memphis had levied a tax on shipments unloaded on the wharf in the city. Some two thousand boatmen were waiting to unload and had refused to pay the tax. The city enlisted the help of the military, and the threat was crushed.

By 1848, the population of the city had increased to almost four thousand residents, and the department was expanded to seven led by a captain. In 1850, Memphis city leaders decided that police were only needed in the evenings, so daylight patrol was abolished. It didn't take long for them to come to their sense and realize the error of their ways, and less than a year after getting rid of daytime police officers, they were reinstituted.

The city was growing, and as it did, the citizens became weary of the large amount of crime that was occurring. A man was murdered in the streets by a well-known card shark. The card shark was retained by locals and held for the police. He was escorted to the jail and locked up. A crowd began to assemble near the jail, and they began to call for the murderer's immediate hanging. Things were quickly getting out of hand when a local man of stature mounted the front steps of the jail and spoke to the crowd. He proclaimed that they could not kill this man because he murdered another. In essence, he said that two wrongs do make a right, and he was able to satisfy the crowd and avert a hanging. This man later became one of the most famous generals for the confederacy during the civil war, Nathan Bedford Forrest.

Memphis was, at that time, full of slaves. These slaves were considered the personal property of their owners. Since slaves could be sold for thousands of dollars, they were extremely valuable to their owners. The owners realized that slaves would sometimes get into trouble while in town, so they arranged with the police force a program whereby any slaves committing assorted crimes would not be shot on sight for their offenses. The police were charged with chasing after the slaves on foot.

The start of the Civil War saw most of the policemen enlist in the army. The city of Memphis was lost to the Federals rather early in the campaign, and after a relatively short period of time, martial law was instituted. The Union army took control of running the city until the cessation of hostilities. After the war ended, some four thousand discharged black soldiers were sent to Fort Pickering in Memphis. They became quite a force in the city and began making bold moves on the white residents. Things came to a head when a white man was shot and killed by a black soldier after he pushed a black boy off a white boy he was in a fight with. Word spread like wildfire and whites within the city began rioting.

The local police begged the Federal army for help. The rioting went on for three days before it ended. Many lives, both black and white, were lost during this tragic event.

From the end of the war in 1865 until 1870, the police department in Memphis was reporting directly to the governor of the state of Tennessee, who was a hated carpetbagger appointed by the president. With no local control of the police, crime ran rampant throughout the city. Murders, rapes, burglaries, assaults became commonplace. The residents begged for help, but their pleas fell on deaf ears. Not until the elections held in 1870 did Tennesseans regain control of their state and force the carpetbaggers out.

First in 1873, then again in succeeding years, Memphis was hit with an epidemic of yellow fever. In the first year alone, some fifty officers were stricken with the dreaded disease, and 20 percent of them died from it. The citizenry did not fare much better. The death rate was staggering, and many people abandoned the city, never to return.

In 1899, one citizen, Joe Knight, known as a local criminal, confronted Sergeant Oliver Hazard Perry in front of the police station. He was angry with Perry and had promised to kill the sergeant. When the sergeant arrived, Knight pulled out a pistol and confronted him. In his rather simple report, Perry wrote "Joe Knight came to the station to kill Sergeant Perry. Knight's funeral will be held tomorrow at 2:00 p.m."

In 1910, the Memphis Police Department received its first two motor vehicles. One was used as an ambulance and the other was a patrol wagon. Most officers at that time patrolled on either horseback or with bicycles. The use of telephones began around this same time.

Memphis purchased its first real pursuit vehicle in 1921. Four men had attempted to rob a Ford Motor Company pay car. The robbers opened fire on the occupants of the car killing two police officers and wounding another. They panicked and jumped into a high-powered Cadillac and began to flee out of town. Another officer had commandeered a local driver's Cadillac and pursued the villains into the suburbs. In Germantown, local residents got word of the pursuit and lay in waiting for the Cadillac containing the robbers. They hid in the brush along Poplar Pike Road when they spotted a Cadillac fast approaching. Regrettably, the Cadillac they spotted was actually the pursuers. As they approached the hidden citizens, they opened fire. A Memphis police lieutenant was killed, and three others in the car were wounded. The robbers were arrested the next day and convicted. This proved to the city fathers that a stronger, reliable pursuit car was needed. They purchased a new Packard with a big engine, and it could hold eight people. They placed armor around the front window to protect the occupants. It could travel up to seventy-five miles per hour when the speed limit at the time was only twenty. Radios were first installed in new police vehicles in 1921.

In 1933, the Memphis Police Department snared one of its most notorious outlaws. George Kelly, also known as Machine Gun Kelly, was arrested and taken into custody in the fall of that year. He had been hiding out in a local area home with his wife and two of his henchmen. He was eventually convicted of kidnapping and sentenced to ninety-nine years at Alcatraz.

The year 1937 saw the opening of the Memphis Police Academy. It was modeled after the famous FBI academy, and the first class of twenty-five men, which represented 10 percent of the department at that time, began. The opening remarks to this new class were made by J. Edgar Hoover, head of the Federal Bureau of Investigation in Washington, DC. One of the first classes held included a program on safe driving. It was taught that on regular patrol, squad cars should not exceed the local maximum speed limit, which was still twenty miles per hour. However, they were permitted to get up to thirty-five miles per hour while en route to a call.

World War II saw many officers take a leave of absence from the department so that they could serve their country. The city obtained additional machine guns to provide them with enough firepower to overcome any saboteurs. Most officers returned to duty after the war ended in 1945, but it did take a number of years afterward for all the returning servicemen to get reinstated with the MPD.

In the succeeding years, Memphis was to be at the forefront of instituting many upgrades, some nationally recognized. Memphis is recognized as being the first city in America to mandate periodic vehicle testing. It bought its first aircraft in 1960, and helicopter usage was not far behind. Training for new officers was steadily increased over the years. From its initial requirement of two weeks, current standards mandate twelve weeks of training to become fully certified.

The most historically significant event in Memphis took place when Martin Luther King Jr. was murdered at the Lorraine Motel in Memphis. He was well protected by the MPD along with his own personal staff. The Lorraine Motel in Memphis was not one of the top-notch motels in the city. Far better known was the Peabody in downtown. This was an elegant hotel where virtually all dignitaries visiting the city were bound to stay. It had been a fixture in the downtown for decades and remains one today. Anyone who has witnessed the famous Peabody ducks can testify to its grandeur. King initially was booked into this great old hotel but changed his plans in order to appear frugal. He was in town in support of sanitation workers who were holding a strike against the city for better wages and working conditions. His murder by a sniper hidden in a bathroom took the city and the nation by complete surprise. This single event led to some of the most violent episodes in the history of the city of Memphis. All leaves for officers were cancelled indefinitely. Officers patrolled in cars that contained as many of them as they could handle, no less than four to a car. A citywide dawn-to-dusk curfew was established. Anyone caught outside after dusk and before dawn was subject to arrest and held in jail. Some officers worked twenty-four hours straight catching a few hours' sleep wherever they could find it. It was not unusual to find officers bunked out in fire stations, police stations, etc. It was sheer pandemonium for the better part of a week. Things only finally settled down once the National Guard was called out. The Memphis Police Department simply did not have the manpower to handle the crisis. No department in America could have done a better job under those circumstances. There were simply not enough of them to go around. Terrible times for all.

There were many more changes within the department in the succeeding years. Today, it is recognized as a top law enforcement agency. The training is second to none, and the personnel are some of the most dedicated people you could ever meet.

CHAPTER 3

The Theft of the Purse

The store where the theft took place had hired one of these off-duty Memphis police officers to work security. He was in full uniform and was well-known in the community. The victim informed this officer about her missing purse, and he immediately called it in to dispatch and began the hunt for a suspect. He had someone in mind, but since no one, including the victim, had actually seen the theft take place, it was, at best, a guess. Security cameras, commonplace today, were years away from being utilized regularly back in 1983. They were far too expensive and cumbersome to use. The cop recalled there had been a local petty criminal hanging around the store, and this off-duty officer immediately suspected he was probably involved.

A patrol car was dispatched to the location to write the report and do the initial investigation. It was a standard two-man unit manned by a couple of longtime Memphis Police Department officers, K. Renfrow and V. J. Mhoon.

They were met outside in the parking lot by the off-duty officer, Patrolman Don Ross, who was working at the store. They asked what he knew about the incident and if he knew who the perpetrator was. He identified a potential suspect who he knew lived not far from the store where the purse snatching took place. Although he could not positively identify anyone, he thought it might be a local subject known by the officer. Ross had been a schoolteacher before joining the police department and had once taught this individual. He had been told by one of the cashiers at the store that this suspect had been hanging around the store all day long, and Ross did recall seeing him in the store. The officers, including Ross, went to the house of the person identified as the possible suspect. He was not home, but his brother was. He told the officers that the man they were looking for (his brother) had not been at the house for the past few days. However, he knew where he was and offered to get him on phone so that the officers could talk to him. The officers took him up on his offer and the call was made. The brother got him on the phone and spoke with him for a few minutes before handing the phone over to one of the officers.

After speaking with the suspect, the officer quickly concluded that he was not the man they were looking for and could not have committed the crime, although he did not mention this to him or his brother. The suspect was extremely irritated over the phone call. He felt that this was nothing more than harassment on the part of the Memphis Police Department.

While he was talking to the suspect over the phone, the officer could hear yelling and obscenities being shouted in the background. He could not make out exactly what was being said, but the officer knew hostility when he heard it. Someone was pretty pissed. Since he was convinced that they had the wrong person, the officer decided not to do anything further with the original suspect after speaking with him on the phone.

After concluding the phone call, the officers thanked the brother for his help and left. They returned to the store to write the incident report. In the report, the officers mentioned the suspect and that they had cleared him from suspicion. It was obvious to them that he could not have possibly committed the crime as he was nowhere near the scene of the crime at the time it happened. At this point, the officers could do little except write the report and turn it in when the shift ended. It was out of their hands and now the responsibility of the detective division to follow up.

CHAPTER 4

Report Taken

When the report eventually wound its way to the detective division, it would have been given a very low priority. Someone most likely would have eventually gotten around to talking with the victim, but very little effort would be put forth in trying to solve this crime. Not because the Memphis Police Department did not want to bother with it, it was simply a matter of priorities. Detectives have many different cases to work on during the course of their shifts. A crime involving a few dollars with no witnesses or any personal injuries simply did not warrant a full court press.

Detectives would investigate, but the chances of solving this crime and recovering the property were nonexistent. They felt that maybe they would recover the purse, but that was about it.

These were the days before video cameras and identity theft. When a purse or wallet was stolen, the only item of much value inside would have been the cash, credit cards, and possibly any personal checks.

Once the victim contacted the credit card companies, the fraud alert would go out, and the card would be cancelled. The victim would be out of cash and that would be the extent of her loss. The banks would be responsible for any fraudulent charges made on the card. Besides the lost cash and any other personal items, all the victim really had to contend with was the aggravation in getting accounts closed. Nowadays, identity theft can create a nightmare for the victims that oftentimes take years to get cleared up. However, back in 1983, no one had ever heard of identity theft. It simply did not exist yet.

CHAPTER 5

Lindberg Sanders

Meanwhile, the man who had talked to the officers was upset that the police were still considering him a suspect. He had spent the entire day, in fact, the past few days, at a home on Shannon Avenue, which was miles away from the grocery store. He had been at the home of Lindberg Sanders along with some thirteen other men. These men were there because Sanders would provide them with free wine, marijuana, and occasionally, a few dollars. In exchange for this, Sanders would preach to his "flock."

Some of his followers took him seriously and were genuinely interested in his teachings, but most just went because Sanders would provide for them. Good jobs were hard to come by in North Memphis and there was not a lot to do, so Sanders's frequent get-togethers gave the men something to do to pass the time. Sanders would preach for hours and hours on end. He had some pretty bizarre teachings that would make some of the nonbelievers chuckle. But since there was not anything better to do, they stayed. They all would listen to him talk, but some were more zealous than others.

There were twelve basic beliefs taught by Sanders. They were the following:

1. Marijuana is an herb and, therefore, a gift from God.
2. Men should never cover their heads, but women should always have their heads covered.
3. Men should not shave nor should have their hair cut.

4. The opinions of women were not worth consideration, and women should not attend religious meetings with men.
5. Cult members should not eat pork or drink clear water: however, Kool-Aid, beer, and wine were acceptable.
6. Police are the devils.
7. White people cannot go to heaven because the Bible was written for black people only.
8. White people are heathens and so are black people who act like white people, such as black police officers and any black that worked with whites.
9. The Ten Commandments are to be obeyed; however, cult members are not to attend any church because the churches are filled with false prophets and hypocrites.
10. Cult members should not shake hands.
11. Physicians are of no value.
12. Bible study should emphasize the Old Testament.

The group had no formal name, printed no literature, practiced no rituals, nor could they be identified by any religious symbols. Some thought that the source of the religious messages may have been from words found in the music of Jamaica known as reggae.

There were no initiations, no dues, or fees paid by anyone at anytime. There was also no outside solicitation of funds by members of this group. Sanders would provide with what little money he was receiving on disability and whatever money his wife would bring home from her job.

The commitment of cult members ranged from those with complete devotion to Lindberg Sanders to those whose main interest was the free marijuana, wine, and small amounts of money that Sanders occasionally provided to his followers. Meetings were not held on any set schedule and were normally held in the home of Lindberg Sanders, although a few meetings were held in other homes. The meetings normally involved drinking wine, smoking marijuana, and reading the Bible.

The cult never numbered more than twenty-five members and had no apparent connection with any other organized group. Members would come and go, but a nucleus of seven to eight men were the core. These were the true believers that found something in his teachings. The members recognized Sanders as the sole leader.

Sanders and his followers had been together for the more than the past twenty-four hours. When the police called for Coleman regarding the purse snatching, it lit a fire under him. Because he thought that this was the first sign of the apocalypse, he berated Coleman for his handling of the call with the police. He felt he was too passive and that he should have been more aggressive in his dealing with the police. That prompted Coleman to call the police back, and this is the call that resulted in Schwill and Hester being dispatched to the location.

Lindberg Sanders was born in a small farming community in Mississippi. After a few years in rural Mississippi, Sanders' mother, Lucille, had had enough of the frustrations of being black and living in Mississippi in the late 1930s. It was one of the poorest counties in one of the poorest states in the Union. It was a hard life with little future or hope. She thought a better life awaited her in a big city. It certainly could not be any worse than what they were living through in Mississippi. It was with this in mind that she left her husband and took her child to Memphis. Lindberg Sanders' father was to remain in Drew, Mississippi, until his death. It is unclear whether or not he ever saw his father again.

City life seemed to agree with the Sanders family. Lindberg grew up attending Hyde Park Elementary School, and he graduated from Manassas High School. He and his future wife had first met at the Hyde Park Elementary School, and they began dating in high school. Shortly after they had graduated, they got married. The marriage would go on to produce five children, Linda, Lucinda, Larnell, Labern, and Lancer. By all accounts, Sanders was a devoted father as the children were growing up. He was particularly proud of his daughter Lucinda. He would often make it a point to drive her to all her school functions. She was to graduate in 1971 and was named Miss Douglass High School.

He also enjoyed time with his sons. He often took them fishing and hunting, just like most fathers in the South. Hunting and fishing are seen as rites of passage to families raised in the South. A boy grows into a man in this part of the country with a hunting rifle in one hand, a fishing pole in the other. The boys would become so excited that usually they would not be able to sleep the night before a trip. They look back at these times with pride and happiness.

After Sanders got married, he needed to provide for his new wife. He got a job working for the city in a job he tolerated, but never really enjoyed. He left after only a couple of years when an opportunity arose in the North to learn a trade. Unions were strong in the Midwest, and the pay was good. The benefits were even better, so Sanders went to Ohio to learn the construction business. It did not take him very long to realize that the Midwest was not the place he wanted to raise his family. It was extremely cold and much more expensive to live in than the South. So after a while, he returned to Memphis and found work at a local meatpacking company. He was making good money, and this allowed him to move his family into a tiny frame home on Hunter Street in Memphis. His job at the meatpacking company was hard, but Sanders was never bothered by hard work, and it was better than any job he had had before. He did not mind the work at all. An honest day's work for an honest day's dollar was important to him. He spent the next nine years working for the packing company. Unfortunately, tough times hit the industry, and the plant closed. Sanders was out of work with a family to support. There were no jobs to be had in meatpacking in Memphis, so he decided to take work where he could find it. He had learned a trade back in Ohio and was able to fall back on the construction business to keep his family afloat. He worked for a local contractor for a time. He also began doing jobs on the side for cash.

In 1962, Sanders moved his family a few blocks away to 2239 Shannon Avenue. All the homes in the neighborhood were similar. Small-frame houses on one level with postage-stamp-sized lots built on a slab foundation. They were built in the late 1940s to capitalize on the returning servicemen from World War II. With Sanders's knowledge of construction, he was able to remodel the home to make it more contemporary. His house would become the envy of all in the neighborhood. He enjoyed doing things around the house. When the quality of the work he did became known throughout the area, he began receiving more and more requests from friends and neighbors to work on their own homes. He was usually willing to help out, but soon grew tired of working side jobs along with his regular full-time job. Sanders seemed particularly drawn to ornamental ironwork. He thought that the more ornamental iron around the house, the classier the house became. Attached to the front of his home were a number of ornamental iron figures. The patio had iron chairs, the house numbers were iron, and the screen door was solid iron and quite heavy. This door would later play an important role in the lives of Robert Hester and Ray Schwill.

However, it was the interior of the home that truly reflected the talents and abilities of Lindberg Sanders. One room featured a full-size circular bed. Ornate faux brick graced one of the interior walls. Z-Brick was becoming very popular in many more upscale homes in the better Memphis neighborhoods, and Sanders's modest home in North Memphis was the only one in the area that had it. A screened-in porch at the back of the house gave Sanders the idea to convert it into a den. He finished the room with a curved bar complete with velvet lining. Shag carpeting was all the rage and Sanders added it in the den. A large mirror was hung behind the bar, and a new stereo was added as the final touch to his creation. Comfortable, tub-style chairs were added to give the room a cozy feeling. Barstools adorned with leather were placed around the bar.

However, in the early 1970s, things began to deteriorate for Sanders. He began to suffer from delusional behavior. He told his wife about what was happening, and she wasn't sure how to deal with it. At first, she believed his stories and was stunned. But after they became more and more bizarre, she realized there was a problem. He had claimed that he was beaten by a local white motorcycle gang. A little while later, he also claimed to have been beaten by members of the Memphis Police Department. He told people that he had been killed by police officers but that God had brought him back to life to serve a purpose. He began to study the Bible, and it wasn't long before he began preaching to anyone that would listen. His wife had convinced him to get help, and he began seeing a professional therapist. He spent some time institutionalized, but it had little impact on him once he was released. He had begun receiving disability checks from the government. His Bible teachings included members of both sexes, but women (usually the wives and girlfriends of the males in attendance) were not encouraged to attend. Oftentimes, the men would be around the house for many hours and sometimes days at a time.

Over time, as Sanders continued his slide downward, his wife attempted to get him committed to an institution once again. She failed, and with this failure went her hopes for the future with Lindberg Sanders. She continued praying that he would start therapy again and maintain his medications. She never gave up hope because she remembered the loving father and husband he had once been. How could such a good man fall into such strange and odd behavior? Fortunately, the kids were grown. Sanders's demons were his alone.

CHAPTER 6

Coleman Calls Dispatch

Michael Coleman called the department at 8:58 p.m. from Sanders's home on Shannon Street. In the tape recording of the call, you can clearly hear Coleman tell the dispatcher that he heard that someone at the department was looking for him in reference to a theft. The dispatcher, who had not been on duty when the original call about the purse snatching went out, was confused and asked Coleman if this had anything to do with a warrant. Coleman repeated "warrant" but then said, "Come by my house and accuse me of stealing something or something."

During this exchange with Coleman, you can clearly hear Lindberg Sanders in the background. He sounds highly agitated, and at one point, he is heard to say "Tell the motherfucker about three minutes ago, five minutes ago, about five minutes ago." The tone of Sanders's voice is highly agitated, almost to the point of being out of control. This information was never relayed to Schwill and Hester when the call was placed dispatching them to 2239 Shannon Street. This is a transcript of the exact call that went out to car 128:

> 128 a complainant at 2239 Shannon, male named Coleman advises he just arrived home and neighbor stated police were there looking for him earlier involving some purse snatch. He is there and wants to get it straightened out. As far as we know it's on the day shift. Have no calls on it ourself. 2239 Shannon.

The dispatcher fails to notify the officers about the threatening voice heard in the background during the phone call from Coleman. In fact, no mention is made of anything regarding a potential problem existing in the home. Sanders's loud shouting into the phone should have alerted the dispatcher to a potential problem, and that information should have been relayed to the officers. This may not have prevented the tragedy, but it most certainly would have made Schwill and Hester more aware of what awaited them. It is one of the many ironic twists in this story that led to tragedy. Had fate intervened, perhaps eight people would still be alive to this day.

When Schwill and Hester knocked on the front door that cold January evening, they had no way to know what awaited them. After all, it was a simple purse-snatching call or so they were told. They were invited inside, and they knew immediately that they were in trouble.

Lindberg Sanders was known around the neighborhood as being rather strange. When he first moved into the home on Shannon Street, he was respected as a talented carpenter and handyman. His home was constantly being remodeled and improved, and he did all the work himself. The intricate pattern tiles he laid on the front porch remain there to this day.

However, over the years, his mental condition steadily deteriorated. Gradually, he began to exhibit some rather odd behavior to his neighbors. He began to tell anyone that would listen that drinking clear water was against the teachings of the Bible. Colored water was acceptable, like Kool-Aid, as was beer and wine. He also believed that pork was a plague on the human race and was to be avoided. His family noticed his odd behavior was getting much worse and pleaded with him to get help. Finally, he agreed and sought help in a free clinic. He was diagnosed and given medications which seemed to help.

When he was taking his medication, he was the old Lindberg Sanders. He was close to his family and a dedicated father. However, the real challenge was to ensure that he remained on his meds. On this fateful day in January, he had been off his medication for a long time. His wife was concerned and tried numerous times to get him committed, but had not been successful in doing so.

January 6 saw another meeting held at the Sanders's home. The usual attendees were there, along with a few of their wives. Meetings held by Sanders at his home for his followers were certainly not unusual. They had occurred countless times in the past. This one, however, was different. Eventually, Sanders ordered the wives to return home.

Dorothy Sanders knew many of the men who regularly attended these meetings. She was familiar with Cassell Harris, James Murphy, and T. C. Smith as they were local neighborhood kids who grew up in the area. Dorothy had left her husband on Christmas Eve and went and stayed at the home of a relative. Lindberg had stopped taking his medication, and unless he agreed to resume his regular prescribed medications, she refused to move back in. She would remain in contact with him always, but she had to do something to force him to get help. She thought leaving him would be enough. Sadly, it wasn't. Late in the first week in January, word had circulated throughout the neighborhood that Sanders had begun to preach about the upcoming apocalypse. This was nothing new for Sanders. His doctor recalled Sanders as one who was constantly holding the Bible and preaching about the end of the world. It's no wonder why Dorothy Sanders wanted him back on his medications.

Dorothy was at the local grocery store on Saturday, the eighth of January when she ran into the wife of T. C. Smith. Mrs. Smith told her that her husband had been at the Sanders's home since Friday and was going to remain there for three days. When Dorothy returned to her new home at her aunt's house, her husband called her. He wanted her to come back to the house on Shannon Street. She replied that she had to wash clothes, and Sanders told her not to worry about the clothes, that she might not even need them. She consented to come over and ended up cooking for all the men in the house.

January 10 saw Andrew "Ju Ju" Houston, Cassell Harris, and another man leave the house on Shannon Street to visit their wives. They were not sure that they would ever see them again and wanted one last visit to say good-bye. Sanders's preachings about the end of the world had made them uneasy, and they were beginning to believe it. Better to say your good-byes while there was still time. Harris told his wife that he was sorry for everything bad that he had done to her. He sought her forgiveness for which she readily gave. Houston gave his wife the keys to the car and told her it was over on Shannon Street, and if she wanted it, she should go and get it. Before the men left, a neighbor overheard part of the conversation. She heard one of the men exclaim that they were going to go to heaven. Then they simply walked away. Both wives had an eerie feeling that day. Ever since the men had been hanging around the Sanders's house, they seemed a little out of sorts. But this was different.

None of them had ever seen their spouses acting so strangely. They knew something was brewing, but had no idea what was happening. They would never see their husbands again. Sanders had grown to hate the police after claiming that they had killed him, and his followers shared this animosity toward authority. He had been enraged by the phone call from the officers investigating the purse snatching. He was enraged not only that the officers called his house, but in the way in which Coleman (the original suspect) handled the call. He felt that he was being too conciliatory toward the police. He was furious that he was cooperating with them at all. He had no way of knowing that the officers had cleared his friend and follower of any involvement in the crime. It probably didn't matter.

Sanders and his followers had been drinking and smoking marijuana for the better part of the day. As the rage inside Sanders grew, he could contain himself no longer. He ordered Coleman to call the police back.

When he did, the dispatcher he eventually spoke with was clearly confused about the call. He knew nothing about the earlier report of the purse snatching. He subsequently dispatched a unit to the address on Shannon Street to follow up. He related to the officers on the call that it had something to do with a purse snatching, and the main suspect wanted to clear the matter up. The dispatcher reported that he had no record of any purse snatching and that it must have occurred during the day shift.

The unit sent was a two-man car. In the car were Patrolmen Ray Schwill and Robert Hester.

As Officers Hester and Schwill arrived on the scene, they had no idea what was awaiting them inside the small-frame home in the reasonably quiet residential neighborhood. When they pulled up in front of the house, everything looked fine. The house was well taken care of, and they could see that whoever lived there took pride in it. Ornate molding trimmed the outside, and the porch had been inlaid with tile that remains there to this day. Inside an elaborate bar had been built by Sanders along with a bedroom that featured a circular mattress and box spring. Orange and green shag carpeting had been found in a number of the rooms. But the demons that possessed the man had become more impossible for him to deal with. He once sought help from a psychotherapist and had been diagnosed as a psychotic. He had deteriorated over the years to the point where he began envisioning the end of the world. Since he was providing wine and marijuana to anyone that attended his teachings, he attracted a young crowd that came primarily to get high. Sanders developed what is loosely described as a cult of followers.

Both officers were experienced members of the Memphis Police Department. Neither knew about the previous call at the grocery store. They were assigned to another area of the city, and their radio was on a different frequency than the radios normally used in this area. Because of this radio frequency issue, the original officers sent to investigate the purse-snatching incident had no way of knowing about a second car being dispatched to Shannon Avenue. In fact, these officers had concluded their investigation of the matter and were writing the report in the parking lot of the grocery store when Schwill and Hester were sent to Shannon Avenue. Had they been able to overhear the radio traffic, they could have, and likely would have, told dispatch to disregard the call as they had already handled the complaint.

CHAPTER 7

Dispatch Sends a Car to Shannon Street

The call Coleman placed to dispatch was filled with pure hatred. Sanders and others could be heard in the background threatening police officers. Dispatchers are trained to weed out any background noise and concentrate on the caller exclusively, but amazingly, none of this information was relayed to the officers when dispatch sent out the call. The call went out as a simple purse snatching. Memphis, not unlike all major metropolitan areas in the United States, sees more than its share of violent crime. Murders, rapes, aggravated assaults, burglaries, etc., Memphis police officers experience the worst crimes imaginable on an all too frequent basis. Every officer is trained to treat each call as a potentially life-threatening incident. Officers are continually taught to never let their guard down. Every call has the potential to quickly denigrate into a life-threatening situation. Fortunately, most don't. It becomes easy for officers to fall into a routine. The vast majority of police officers go their entire career and never have to fire their guns at an offender. Many officers serve over twenty years and never even have to draw their weapon while on duty. There is a natural hierarchy into the way that police officers treat calls. The more violent the crime, the more aware the responding officers become. The adrenaline begins pumping and heart rates increase on calls of this sort.

Assault, rape, and murder calls generate the highest degree of attention. Domestic disturbances also create a sense of dread in most officers. It is simply not possible for every officer to be at the optimum level of alertness on every call. Purse snatchings are as routine as shoplifting calls. There is very little danger associated with them. Most likely the offender is a common, petty criminal who has been in and out of prison for years and is well-known to the experienced officers. More likely a drug addict who has to steal in order to feed his or her habit. Subsequently, when officers respond to a routine call, they usually view it as just another incident report that will need to be written. It is the responsibility of the dispatcher to give the most reliable information possible when sending the officers to any call. Dispatchers know this, and yet oftentimes, they fail to relay to the officers key information that could save lives. The relationship between officers and dispatchers in most departments is strained. It is more than a simple rivalry between two departments within an organization. Many dispatchers see themselves as being as important as cops themselves, and there can be resentment within their ranks because they are normally paid less than officers. Cops see themselves as being on the firing line and therefore believe they deserve more. The truth is that both are integral to the success in maintaining a city's security. Either way, both departments are critical to modern law enforcement.

Both officers and dispatchers are trained to keep radio traffic at an absolute minimum.

The logic behind this policy is sound. An officer or dispatcher rambling on with some minor call might make an emergency call wait. While the radio is in use, other parties are unable to broadcast. Sometimes, the individual sending out the radio call, if he keys the microphone at the same time someone else does, then that person may not even know that his broadcast was received. This is true of both the dispatcher and the cop in his car.

The problem a policy of keeping broadcasts to a minimum creates is that key details may be neglected or left unreported that may be critical to the safety of the officer assigned to the call. A tragedy may ensue, and it places lives in danger when critical details are not relayed to the officers who need the information the most. Whether it is complacency or a fear of being on the air too long, it can create an environment whereby lives could be put in jeopardy. A rare occurrence to be sure, but a most dangerous one nonetheless.

Police patrol work has been described by many as being 99 percent of utter boredom punctuated by times of sheer excitement, fear, anger, and heart-pumping activity.

Patrolling in a police car may seem to the public to be exciting, and at times, it certainly can be; but after driving around your sector or district time and time again, it gets pretty routine. But at least, police officers are out doing something. They can make traffic stops whenever they get the urge. They can patrol in areas where the public seldom goes. They have the capability to make the shift as busy or slow as they wish to a certain degree. They have a lot of latitude to influence how busy they are. Naturally, a lot of this depends upon the amount of calls they may be sent to.

Dispatchers, on the other hand, are restricted to sitting behind a desk the entire shift. There is not a lot that they can do make the time go by any faster.

Dispatchers are trained to ask questions, to interrogate callers over the phone to attempt to provide the officers with as much critical information as they can. For example, if a call comes in regarding a domestic complaint, dispatchers are trained to ask if there are any weapons involved, if both subjects are still on the premises, if has there been any drinking or drug use, etc. However, in spite of this training, when boredom strikes, occasionally dispatchers can fail to ask the right questions, or if they do, they alone have to make a split-second decision in terms of what information to relay to the officers being sent to the scene. When officers are sent on a call and they feel they need additional information, they are not shy about requesting more details from the dispatcher. It is because of this that dispatchers and officers often have a strained relationship in many departments. This does not happen all the time, but it does occasionally create a problem.

However, in Shannon Street, the call was pretty simple, a routine purse-snatching call, not a violent crime where lives could be at stake. Oh, how wrong they were.

CHAPTER 8

The Assault Begins

It is not clear if this was the situation that Officers Schwill and Hester were facing when they were dispatched at 2100 hours that fateful night. Certainly, there is little doubt that something was wrong with the dispatch as it was relayed to them. The dispatcher was clearly confused about the call, and vital information was not passed along to the officers albeit unintentionally. When Sanders called complaining about the police interrogating Coleman as a possible purse snatcher, you could hear loud screaming in the background. The voices in the background were shouting about killing police officers and threats were clearly heard being shouted in the background. None of these were ever relayed to the officers. It appears as if the dispatcher was concentrating on other issues, like trying to find out what the caller was referring to. No doubt there was confusion on the part of the dispatcher who was clearly baffled.

When the cops arrived, they were under the impression that they were going on a simple routine call. Had they known about the screaming in the background during the phone call, they certainly would have been better prepared to face the danger. If it would have changed the ultimate outcome is anyone's guess. But Schwill and Hester most certainly would have approached the call more cautiously. Why the dispatchers failed to advise Officers Schwill and Hester of the obvious dangers they were walking into is a mystery.

When Schwill and Hester arrived on the scene, they radioed dispatch notifying the department where they were. They received the original call from dispatch at 2100 hours. They arrived on the scene at 2104, and at 2106, they radioed for backup. Things had gone bad quickly. At 2107, another call, more frantic, came from the officers seeking help. This call was a frantic scream that everyone who could hear was made under extreme duress. Many officers monitoring their radios heard the pleas for assistance. Most officers will only call for backup under the direst of circumstances or if they believe the situation could turn bad. The macho attitude is still prevalent in most departments. For these two officers to call not once, but twice, sent the message to the others responding that things were turning bad and quickly. Help was on the way. What Hester and Schwill encountered when they arrived on the scene was totally unexpected. They were under the impression that they would simply be interviewing a possible suspect about a purse snatching. When they knocked on the door and were invited inside the home, they found it poorly lit inside. They could not see very well, but they sensed very quickly that this was not going to be another "report taken" call. Inside the home were at least fourteen men. They could sense the tension in the room immediately. Feeling trouble brewing, they knew they had to extricate themselves from the closed confines of the house. Inside the small house, they could easily become trapped with no room to maneuver. They needed to get outside for a number of different reasons. The radios, their lifeline to the department, worked better outside, and they would be closer to the safety and security of their squad car. They told the subject, Michael Coleman, to come outside and they could get the matter straightened out. He agreed, and as he got up to go outside, Lindberg Sanders jumped up and began to follow the men outside. This action by Sanders prompted the others in the room to also follow. The cops were outnumbered seven to one, and they knew they were in trouble. That's when the first call for backup went out. Police officers are constantly trained to handle situations like this, and the first thing they are taught is to try to calm everyone down and to take command of the situation. However, they were also trained to not lose control, and this was normally done by maintaining an aggressive posture. Dominating others would create the impression that they were in charge. Police academy training mandated control, and Schwill and Hester followed their instincts. This control by intimidation usually is effective, but when you're facing large numbers of hostiles, a more prudent approach would be to attempt to play down the aggressiveness. Second-guessing is easy to do. Schwill and Hester had moments to react. Decisions had to be made instantly, and their training led them in a particular direction. That's another reason they wanted the main subject outside the home. They were attempting to defuse a rapidly deteriorating situation, and a common effective method to do this was to gain control of the situation and to separate the people involved. This is a common tactic used in virtually all domestic disputes.

When all the players moved outside with the officers, they only became more agitated. Mob mentality took over, and their sheer numbers made them, as a group, much more aggressive. They cops wanted Coleman outside, and they were not expecting the others to follow. As Schwill led Coleman outside the home on the front lawn, the first blow was struck. He was punched in the face by another man who had followed them out the front door. His partner, Hester, was standing near the front doorway. He had allowed Schwill to take command in the handling of the situation and was following his lead. Things only got worse. The mob mentality began to take even more control of the crowd. It was at this time that the second call for help came from Patrolman Schwill, and the assaults began. As Schwill attempted to take Coleman into custody, he was jumped by a number of men. He had succeeded in getting outside away from the confining interior of the home, but this only delayed things.

Hester had seen what was happening to his partner, but he was overtaken within seconds of Schwill. He was near the main doorway when he was overwhelmed and ended up being dragged back inside the house. Schwill could hear his partner yelling for help, but he needed help himself.

Being hopelessly outnumbered, things turned ugly in a hurry for the officers. Schwill was trying to get his service revolver out of its holster. As he was removing it, someone yelled that he was getting his gun, and his arm was pinned. The gun was forcibly wrenched from Schwill's grasp. In the struggle for the gun, the next thing Schwill felt was searing hot pain in his hand. He had lost his weapon and was now at the mercy of an angry, vicious mob. He could still hear his partner yelling for help, but he was powerless to do anything. He had already been shot once in his hand, and the worst was yet to come. He was in the fight of his life. Once he lost his weapon, he was at the mercy of fanatics who were beating him and Hester unmercifully. As he struggled to regain the momentum, he heard his partner scream, "They got me, Ray" and "Ray, come help me."

He was dragged back into the house, and he saw, through the fog of the beating and while struggling to remain conscious, his partner being dragged into a side room off the main entrance. He was going to do whatever he could to save both himself and his partner. Against overwhelming odds, Schwill got up on his hands and knees and was struggling to stand up when the gun went off again. He was brutally shot for the second time, this time in the head, which knocked him back to the floor. The bullet entered behind his left ear and exited in his lower jaw. Blood was pouring out from this grievous-looking wound.

While the injury was significant, it was not life threatening if he got help quickly, but neither Schwill nor his attackers had no way to know this at the time. Schwill collapsed to the floor and pretended to be dead. This action, no doubt, was instrumental in saving his life.

His partner was dragged, still fighting against huge odds, into a bedroom off toward the side of the residence. Schwill could hear him screaming for help, but he was being watched by Sanders and other men who were uncertain if he was dead. He had to continue the masquerade if he had any hope for survival. He was stunned after being shot twice with his own revolver, and he was fighting for his life. He had no idea how serious his wounds were but he could feel the blood flowing out of his wounds, and he knew he had to get out of there. Shock was a potential problem, and he knew he had to continue playing dead if he had any chance to make it out of this. If he were to go into shock, then the men watching him might be able to see his chest rise and fall when he was breathing. He couldn't let that happen. He knew help was on the way, and he had to stay alert until it arrived. In his mind, which was racing, he was trying to work out a scenario that would allow him to escape his captors. Certainly, he was frightened. He wondered why he and Hester were so viciously attacked. Survival mode had set in, and there would be time for reflection later. He feared that the only way he could get away would be to rely on the other officers he knew were on their way.

Little did he know that help was, indeed, on the way, but that assaulting the house to secure their rescue would not happen for a long, long time. Much too late for most of the men inside. As he lay there in a pool of his own blood, wondering when the next bullet would strike, many thoughts went through his mind. Predominant among them was how in the hell they were going to get out of this jam. When the opportunity arose and he could escape, he was determined to be ready.

CHAPTER 9

Hester Profile

Robert Hester graduated from the Memphis Police Academy in 1973. The academy would later be named in honor of the police director at time the Shannon Avenue murder took place, John Holt. When rookies leave the academy, they normally spend an extended period of time working with seasoned patrol officers called field training officers. Hester and his FTO were on routine patrol duty on May 21, 1973. Hester had only been on the street for a few short weeks, and he had much to learn. He wanted to fit in, and he was working hard to become the best he could be. His training was progressing as expected. His partner was bringing him along slowly as he did with all rookies. It was better to work them slowly into the mundane, paperwork-filled, day-in-day-out routine of police officers employed by the city of Memphis. Rookies or probationary police officers were usually given all the crappy details, and Bobby Hester had more than his fair share of them. They got to do all the paperwork. The academy teaches officers the book. FTOs teach officers the real world. What works best on the street is rarely taught in the academy. Instead, recruits receive textbook training. They are taught how to drive a patrol car, how to write a report, how to shoot well enough to meet the basic requirements. They even receive training that teaches them when to shoot. Once out on the street, it quickly becomes apparent to all rookies that what they learned in the academy was not of much practical use in the real world. In the academy, you are trained to become prolific in hitting a target. On the streets, it's a little more demanding as you quickly find out that the targets in the real world actually shoot back.

Hester had served in the military for two years prior to becoming a Memphis police officer. He enjoyed the military atmosphere, the discipline, but most of all, the camaraderie in the service and found the police department to offer many of the same benefits. The police department also offered a good career path. After twenty years, there were retirement options. In the Memphis Police Department, if one remained on the job after thirty years, you were given an automatic promotion to the rank of captain. This was to reward officers for staying on the job. It was a win-win situation for everyone. The officer gets to retire with the full benefits of a captain. The department and community gets the experience of a seasoned veteran who might have retired years earlier. A great deal for everyone. This program was eliminated a few years ago as being too expensive to maintain. While Hester and his partner were on routine patrol that spring day in 1973, neither knew that the events of what was going to take place that day would go down in Memphis history as one of the bloodiest this river town would ever experience.

Many cops rely on the uniform to command respect. Still others perfect a "don't mess with me" look when on the job. This was not the way Officer Hester did his job. Hester had a natural talent in having people trust him. He was not a big guy, standing only five feet seven inches tall and weighing no more than 150 pounds. Some men of this small stature take on a Napoleonic persona. Being this diminutive, it is hard to intimidate people with your physical presence. So some become more aggressive and loud to compensate for their physical shortcomings. Hester never had this problem. Sure, he was small in stature, but when he spoke, you became aware that here was someone special. He had a genuine concern for his fellow man and people he came in contact with could sense this. Later in his career, as he patrolled some of the most crime-ridden, drug-infested areas of the city, many residents would comment on how Officer Hester seemed genuinely interested in helping them. He had an inbred natural charisma that drew people to him. As a rookie officer, he was somewhat clumsy. Many rookies inherit this rather troubling tendency. You just get out of the academy where your instructors come across as godlike figures. You take every morsel of advice they give you and implant it in your brain. As graduation draws near, you can't wait to get out on the street to prove to your classmates, instructors, and yourself that you belong. That you are as good as what they trained you to be. Once out there, paired up with a seasoned veteran, it quickly becomes clear that maybe things are not as they seemed when you were in the academy. This tends to create clumsiness on the part of the new cop as he is torn between what he was told in the academy and with the realities of the street. He becomes wracked with indecision, and until he gets over it, he will never become a good cop. Most do in a very short time. Officer Hester certainly did.

On Monday, May 21, 1973, a call went out from dispatch about a shooting that had occurred in the 1700 Block of Kansas Street. At that time, this area was not a particularly dangerous one. The call went out at 2:50 p.m. The day shift was set to go off duty in ten minutes.

Patrolman Dave Clark and his partner Joe Cottingham immediately headed toward the call. Upon arrival, they witnessed a scene of horror that neither had ever experienced before. The bodies of four people were strewn all over the street. They also found a federal probation officer, James Crawford, lying critically wounded in the gutter. Clark saw a suspect running away from the scene and gave chase. He chased him on foot to a small shotgun-style ranch house at 1760 Kansas Street. Clark took note that the suspect was armed with what appeared to be a 30/30 caliber rifle. This is a very potent weapon that most police-issued bulletproof vests would do little to stop a round from penetrating. The officer screamed for him to stop, and when he didn't, he fired a round at him, striking him in the shoulder. He knew he had wounded the subject and thought he would surrender quickly. He then sought cover near the corner of a similar frame home. The suspect saw Officer Clark as he sought cover and returned fire, unleashing a shot from his high-powered rifle. He was wounded, but still, he managed to return fire. The round struck the officer in the side of the head, killing him instantly. He never knew what hit him. The suspect, David Sanders, thirty, entered the house after shooting Officer Clark. Other officers surrounded the home, and when he emerged, rifle pointing at the officers, they unleashed a volley of shots at him, killing him. Sanders had shot and killed no less than six people, including the Memphis police officer. Five of these six ended up in the morgue.

This was the call that rookie Officer Hester and his partner were responding to. They sped to the scene on Kansas Street as fast as they could, exceeding speeds in excess of a hundred miles per hour. Hester and his partner arrived on the scene just as the suspect was entering the house. They parked behind a small hill, which, from the top, would give them a great look at the property. As they crawled up the hill, Hester's heart was pounding in his chest. This was his first emergency call, and he was determined to do everything right.

He had been out on the street for a few months, but he knew in this situation he was in way over his head. He didn't know what to do, so he looked to his FTO for guidance.

Shortly after reaching the top of the hill, Officer Hester was anxiously watching his partner's actions. His FTO was busy concentrating on the scene below him, so he told Hester to lie low and stay out of the way.

He saw him draw his weapon, and as he reached down to his side, he was shocked to find that his weapon was nowhere to be found. He panicked and didn't know what to do. He did not want to let on to this veteran officer that he had lost his gun. He would never hear the end of it, and it could be enough to have him fired. The academy had never trained him for this. Frantically searching for his weapon, he noticed something lying at the bottom of the hill. It was his department-issued .38-caliber revolver. Other officers had ascended the same hill, and all were watching the house. All of them had their guns drawn except for Bobby Hester. His was lying at the foot of the hill. He would joke about it later with his friends and family, but the incident left an indelible mark on his psyche. He would never let this happen again.

Afterward, he would constantly be seen patting his holster to ensure that his gun was still there. Officer Hester's first life-threatening call involved a suspect named Sanders. Ten years later, the names Sanders and Hester would become intertwined once again, and the city of Memphis would never be the same again.

Hester was born in 1949 in Alabama. His father worked for the railroad, and when he was offered a promotion that required a transfer to Memphis, he leapt at the chance to provide his family a better life. The family moved into a small-frame home that backed up to the Nonconnah Creek, which wound around a heavily wooded area. Hester would spend hours and hours in these woods hunting and fishing. Much like Lindberg Sanders and his sons, Hester's dad would take him on trips to learn how to hunt and fish. His mother said that his father would take him on hunting and fishing trips beginning when he was seven years old. He would stay up all night just to make certain that he would be awake when his father was ready to leave. He didn't want to risk missing a trip with his dad. Hester graduated from Overton High School in Memphis in 1967. Hester attended Memphis State University for two years and also spent time studying computer science at the state tech but found that career boring. Vietnam was sapping the youth of America, and Bobby Hester and his brother Jerry took their physicals the same day. They were brought up to believe that they had to do their part in the military. His brother was rejected by the army, but Bobby entered the army and spent two years and became a military policeman.

It would be his first introduction as an adult into the world of law enforcement.

When Hester returned from the army in 1972, he was a man without a plan. Not sure of what he wanted to do, he spent the summer driving back and forth between Alabama and home, fishing and hunting. He was in no hurry to begin a career. Jobs were tight, and since he had some money put away, he could afford to take his time seeking employment. Late that summer, his brother had to be hospitalized. Bobby stayed close to home helping the family any way he could. On one of his frequent trips to the hospital, Hester met a lovely young lady who was a friend of his brothers. Before long, Hester needed a job because he and Anita planned on getting married. His father tried to get him a job with the railroad, but a problem emerged with his back. The railroad had an antiquated policy that stemmed back to the days of the Wild West regarding tailbones. If you had a curved tailbone, you could not work on the railroad. No problem if you wanted to be a cop, but the railroad had some very old, obsolete rules. The railroad job was out. So he ultimately decided to go back to the career path he had taken in the military, law enforcement. He got an application for the MPD and filled it out at the kitchen table in his parents' home. He turned in the application to the Memphis Police Department, and on February 26, he entered the academy. A month later, he and Anita married. Two months after his marriage, he graduated from the academy and began his career as a member of the Memphis Police Department.

After joining the Memphis Police Department, Hester spent time working various undercover assignments. Hester did not look like a cop. He was too small, so he was able to penetrate various locations like the glut of topless bars that ringed the city. He spent time on the vice squad working undercover on prostitution stings. Hookers took one look at him and quickly decided that he was not a threat to them. No way this guy could be a cop. Many went to prison shaking their heads trying to figure out where the cops found this guy. He looked like a high school chess team member. After a period of time, Hester became too well-known and was forced to leave his undercover duty.

CHAPTER 10

Hester Taken Hostage

No less than ten to twelve people were with Officer Hester in the side bedroom. His hands were secured behind his back with his own handcuffs. The cuffs were placed so tightly on his wrists that his hands and wrists quickly turned blue due to the lack of circulation. He begged them to loosen them, but they were not interested in his comfort. He was being punched, kicked, slapped, and more. Blows were coming at him from every direction. As soon as the officers were dragged back into the house, seven of the original fourteen men inside ran out the rear of the building. This evened the odds a little bit in the favor of the officers, but they had not been aware of this. By this time, they had been overwhelmed and were in no position to do anything against the seven men left in the house. The men who ran out the rear of the house had decided to save themselves and wanted no part of what was taking place inside. As it turned out, not a single one of these men were prosecuted for the events that took place that fateful January evening. One was arrested, and he happened to be the one who first struck the officer in the doorway as he admitted later. He was given a public defender, who happened to be one of the best the city had to offer, and eventually, all charges against him were dropped. This attorney later became the mayor of Shelby County, Tennessee, which includes the city of Memphis. This same prosecutor would later resign his post as the mayor of Shelby County and be sworn in as the new mayor of the city of Memphis.

CHAPTER 11

Help Arrives

There had been stress and tension building throughout the day within the house, and it exploded into violence once the officers showed up. The men had been in the house listening to the ramblings of Lindberg Sanders, drinking wine, and smoking grass. There had been little sleep among the men, and the circumstances were ripe for violence. Sanders was a diagnosed a psychotic whose mental health had gradually deteriorated over the years. He needed to take his medication to control his erratic behavior, but he began believing that the medication was the work of the devil and that it was controlling him. His neighbors were used to his strange behavior and his insane ramblings. Nailed to an enormous tree within feet of the front door was a poster featuring a pig with the words "Wanted for Murder, Mr. Hog" written in bloodred underneath. This poster had led officers who responded to Hester and Schwill's calls for help to believe that Mr. Hog referred to police officers, who, back in those days, had commonly been referred to as pigs. One officer, Ed Vidulich, was one of the first groups of officers responding to the cry for help, and he spent hours behind that tree during the hostage negotiations. His nickname was Big Ed, and even though he was a large man, this tree offered him protection from the gunfire that had erupted inside.

Meanwhile, Schwill, who had originally radioed for help shortly after arriving on scene, continued to play dead. All he could hear was his partner screaming in the other room. He knew that help was on the way, but had no way of knowing when they would arrive, but he knew it would be soon. He was bleeding profusely from the wounds he sustained, and he was beginning to weaken. If he did not make his move soon, it would be too late. Suddenly, gunfire erupted near the back room where Hester was being held. Sanders, who had been standing over Schwill and had most likely been the one who shot him in the head, ran into the back room to see what was happening, and the other man guarding Schwill bolted to a window and peered outside. The front door was partially open, but the heavy iron screen door was closed. This open door partially blocked Schwill from the view of the other subject. Schwill did not have much time to evaluate his next move. Through vision distorted by blood streaming out of his head wound, he saw his chance. He had been preparing for this move ever since being shot the second time. He knew this might be the only chance he would get so he decided to make his move. With the gunfire coming from the rear of the house commanding the attention of almost everyone inside the house, he jumped up and staggered as fast as he could toward the front door, which was only a few feet away. He forced his shoulder into the heavy iron door and stumbled out onto the porch where other officers were waiting. He was quickly rushed out of harm's way to a waiting squad car out near the curb. An ambulance was ordered to the scene to transport Officer Schwill to the hospital, but the officer in the driver's seat took immediate action. Deciding that Schwill needed help immediately and could not wait for the ambulance to arrive, he floored the Dodge Diplomat and turned on his lights and siren. He was going to get Schwill to the closest hospital. There was no time to wait. A few short minutes later, his car arrived at the hospital. Officer Schwill was rushed inside the emergency room where his clothes were cut off. He was conscious, but in a tremendous amount of pain. The doctors needed to clear all the blood away so that they could evaluate his injuries. These doctors had seen many different gunshot wounds over the years, but they had never witnessed a police officer in this kind of condition. They were determined to do everything they could to save his life. Now there was only one officer left inside to save. Officer Bobby Hester.

CHAPTER 12

Tommy Turner

Being a police officer makes you part of a fraternity. Oftentimes, not without some degree of justification, the prevailing attitude is "It's us against them" especially when dealing with the criminal element. This attitude permeated all the way down to the general public. Cops had often heard people issued traffic citation complain about them. In virtually every incident where the public and police officers intertwine, the officers see the absolute worst that person can be. It's never good news when John Q. Public has to deal with a police officer. Whether it is simply getting a ticket or being told of an accident involving a loved one, the cops always see the worst. When you are exposed to the worst society has to offer day after day, it becomes only natural to form a bond with others within the fraternity. Only other police officers can truly understand what it takes to enforce the law in the community. Officers are suspicious of outsiders and trust only those who wear the blue uniform. Some deal with it better than others, but all feel it. It is a bond similar to the one those who have been in combat together feel. Most embrace it and ranks will quickly close against outsiders.

When Officer Tommy Turner heard the initial call for help, none of this was running through his mind. All he knew was that there were officers in trouble, and he was close enough to the scene to help quickly. When he arrived, he immediately ran the short distance from the curb to the front door of the house and was joined there by the second car to arrive on the scene containing Officers R. Watson and M. Carr. It was eerily quiet. None of the officers could hear anything, and Turner wondered out loud if they had the right address. Watson confirmed they had the right house, and Turner slowly pulled open the heavy iron screen door and kicked the front door in an attempt to gain entry. His kick failed so Watson then tried without success. Turner gained better leverage and kicked the door again, and this time, it flew open. He took a step into the building and saw a man with a gun in his hand run into another room. This stopped him cold. It was the last thing that he expected to see. While this threat was running through his mind, his eyes were searching for the missing cops. He thought he saw the lower pants legs of an officer's uniform and went to his knees while still in the doorway. It was this officer's actions that helped allow Schwill to eventually escape because it opened the main door for him so that all he had to contend with in his escape was the storm door. Had the heavy interior door remained closed, it is doubtful Officer Ray Schwill would have been able to get both it, and the heavy iron storm door opened without being noticed. Meanwhile, Officer Turner had drawn his weapon. As he entered the room, another subject ran into the room and fired a shot in his direction. Turner was about to return fire when he felt a crashing blow to the back of his head. He was knocked off balance and struck again. He aimed his weapon at the subject and pulled the trigger. The gun would not fire because during the assault his weapon had the cylinder knocked loose and was in the reloading position making the gun impossible to fire. He witnessed three men running through the room and drew a bead on them, but the gun still would not fire. He was battling a number of different subjects from different directions and his gun would not fire. Turner was losing consciousness and staggered back out of the house. He stumbled all the way to the cover of a van parked in the driveway. He did not know if he had been shot or not, but he knew he was injured. But he also knew that two of his fellow officers were inside and needed his help, and he was determined to do whatever he could to get them out of there. While behind the cover of the van, Turner saw a brick lying on the ground. With blood pouring out all over his uniform, he picked it up and cautiously approached the front of the house. He threw it through the front window in an effort to get a better view of the inside. All the lights inside had been turned off, and he still could not see anything. At about that time, he heard shots coming from inside the house. Hearing the gunfire erupt, and not knowing in which direction they were coming from, he retreated once again to the relative safety of the van parked in the driveway. All during this time, Turner was fading in and out of consciousness. He had lost a lot of blood and was ordered to the hospital for treatment to his head wound. At the hospital, Turner received numerous stitches. When the treatment was completed, he returned to the scene to offer whatever assistance he could to save his fellow officer. He felt that it was his responsibility to rescue his brother officers and that staying in the hospital was not an option. He most likely had suffered a brain concussion, but it was going to take a lot more than that to keep him away from the scene. He was ordered to leave and was driven to his home to recuperate. Officer Tommy Turner was but one of the many heroes of Shannon Street that day. He displayed the courage required of police officers and without regard for his own safety he did what he had to do.

CHAPTER 13

Russ Aiken

Another officer, Russ Aiken, an eight-year veteran of the Memphis Police Department, also heard the call for help and rushed to the scene. When the call came, Aiken was having dinner nearby at his parents' home. Aiken was riding with a rookie police officer at that time, Cedric Canada, and he would often take rookies with him when he would stop by his parents' house. It was one of the methods he would use to make the rookie feel like part of a team. It also gave him the opportunity to see how the rookie handled himself while away from the job.

Aiken, his partner, and others arrived at the scene within minutes of each other, and a plan was quickly formulated to rescue the two officers they knew were trapped inside the dwelling. They had no idea what awaited them when they arrived on the scene. A lieutenant had arrived moments before Aiken, and since he would be the ranking officer, he was to have taken command. Meanwhile, Aiken had ordered his rookie partner to remain under cover. Two officers were already in the front of the home with the lieutenant so Aiken went around the back to enter from the rear as Officer Tommy Turner was to be the first to enter through the front. Aiken could hear shouts coming from inside the house, but could not make out what was being said. He knew that Officers Schwill and Hester were there, he had noticed their squad car parked in front of the home, and hadn't that been Officer Schwill on the radio calling for help? Where were they? He had no idea, but he felt pretty confident that they were somewhere inside. As he crossed over the porch on his way to the rear, he noticed an officer's police-issue handheld radio lying on the front lawn. It was odd to see it simply lying there as officers were personally responsible for their equipment, including the radio. If it turned up missing, they were going to be held personally responsible for it. He briefly wondered what it was doing there, but quickly put it out of his mind. He had a job to do, and nothing was going to stand in the way of him doing everything he could to rescue the officers inside. None of the officers on the scene had trained together for this scenario, but they instinctively knew what to do. Action was needed, and it was needed immediately if they were going to rescue the two officers trapped inside. When Aiken went around the rear of the structure, he could hear more yelling and muffled screams coming from inside the home. As he approached the rear, he saw a large garbage can standing near the rear doorway. He hesitantly looked inside because it was large enough to hold someone within its confines. It was the only time this night that he hesitated doing anything. He also noticed that the back door was wide open. It was very cold, and there was little light coming from inside. He positioned himself outside the rear door and prepared to make entry. He was awaiting the arrival of more officers to help him, but time was running out. He had drawn his service revolver, and after a few seconds, he bulled through the doorway and saw a scene that he would never forget. He saw, what he assumed to be, Officer Schwill's legs, and they were kicking about near the front of the house in the bedroom entryway. Two men were standing over Schwill, and Aiken frantically radioed dispatch and other officers on the scene that "They were beating him." He then heard two shots and radioed a second time, "They're shooting him." The shooter had heard Aiken, so he then turned his attention toward him and began firing as he advanced rapidly in his direction. Aiken quickly returned fire hitting the man closing in on him, who later turned out to be Lindberg Sanders. Then gunfire exploded to his left side, and he quickly realized he was taking fire from more than one location in the house. His revolver only had a capacity of six rounds, and he had to turn in the direction of this latest threat and return fire. He was quickly out of ammunition. He retreated and leaped over a counter landing on the other side on his back, near the rear door and rolled outside. As this was going on and he was taking fire from two different directions inside the home, he had only one thought, and that was that he knew where the officers were being held hostage, and if he could get back inside quickly, he could rescue them. As he escaped out the back door, he saw one of the subjects that he was trading fire with, down on the floor still shooting, and he was convinced that his shots had found their mark. He wondered how or why he could keep shooting at him because he knew that he had hit him with his first shot.

Now he was outside the house and out of the direct line of fire. Although the thin wall of the home offered little protection against bullets, at least it took him out of the line of sight of the men inside. The lieutenant had moved around to the rear of the house to get a better feel for the layout of the property when Aiken emerged. He gave Aiken a handful of additional pistol rounds. Aiken quickly reloaded his weapon. Without hesitation, he charged headlong back into the doorway and began firing again. He had no time to think over his options. He had to get back inside and help the trapped officers. There was a large plate glass mirror on the wall in the den behind Aiken. In the reflection of this mirror, he thought he was able to hit another one of the subjects, wounding him, but again, ran out of ammunition. In the mirror, he saw the man he was firing at wince in pain as he was turning toward the safety of the backyard. He needed time to reload. In the heat of a gun battle, it does not take long to empty a six-shot revolver. It is one of the reasons that police departments today carry semiautomatic handguns as their duty weapons. Memphis police officers have carried semiautomatics for years. They are simple to re-load (simply eject the magazine and insert a new one). Each magazine can hold up to twelve to fifteen rounds (depending upon the type of gun) giving officers the capability to carry thirty six to forty-five rounds instead of only twelve to eighteen common with the standard six-shot revolver in use at the time. Schwill and Hester, as all officers employed by the MPD in 1983, carried six-shot revolvers with six rounds in the chamber, and they each had holders on their belts that would hold an additional twelve rounds of .38-caliber ammunition. To load this revolver would take some time. Speed loaders which would inject six rounds into the chamber in one motion would have helped, but they were not standard issue at the time. Each round would have to be manually inserted in the chamber by the officer one at a time. This is not as easy as it sounds, and in the heat of battle, as your adrenaline is pumping, it is nearly impossible to do quickly. Compare this to simply pushing a button to eject a magazine and slamming a replacement in its place. Police departments in the twenty-first century have almost exclusively gone to semiautomatic handguns for their officers due to the obvious advantages. No one knows if semiautomatic weapons would have made a difference or not. On the positive side, Aiken would have had far more rounds to fire as he assaulted the house. He could have reloaded much more quickly, and this would have given him a distinct advantage. On the other hand, Sanders and his crew would have also had more rounds at their disposal.

Realizing more clearly what he was up against, he again rolled onto his back and leapt up over the counter and ran back outside. He encountered another officer near the garbage can out back who was carrying a shotgun. He took the shotgun from the officer and asked him how many rounds he had in the weapon. The officer told him that there were four rounds. Aiken told him to remain by the rear door and to cover him. He never saw this officer again. He simply vanished. As Aiken ran back to the rear of the building, he was chambering additional rounds into the shotgun. He needed more firepower than his revolver could give him, and this shotgun was just the weapon he needed. The sound that a shotgun makes when discharged is very loud. It has a distinctive noise, and in the confined space in the home, even the sound of a shotgun round simply being chambered can be very intimidating. Shotguns being fired in the small confines of the house give off an explosive roar. Handguns are loud in confined spaces particularly, but nothing compares to the enormous sound of a shotgun being fired. It can be very intimidating not only by its huge size, but also by the enormous sound it makes when fired. When he re-entered the house, he came under fire once again. The plate glass mirror behind Officer Aiken exploded from the rounds being fired in his direction. When he was later interviewed and asked to identify, by the sound, the types of weapons that were being used against him, he replied that he thought there were many different caliber of weapons being used. To this day, Aiken insists that he heard the distinctive sounds of different caliber weapons being fired in his direction. The only weapons found after the event was all over were the two revolvers carried by Schwill and Hester. Was Aiken mistaken or did something happen to the other weapons he claimed to have heard? Or in the heat of the moment, did Aiken mistake the various weapons used against him incorrectly? As other officers reported that they heard the sounds of different caliber weapons being used to fire on them, one suspects that Aiken was correct. Many different police officers, all highly trained professionals with many years of experience in the use and handling of weapons, wrote later in their statements that they heard the sounds of assorted caliber weapons being used against them.

After his third entry into the house, he exited the building, again in search of additional ammunition. He ran into another MPD officer and told this officer that with his help he was convinced that the two of them could rescue the officer still inside being held hostage. He could sense that he was close to finally getting to them. This officer was a respected member of the department that Aiken knew very well. He was a casual friend of his. Certainly, he could rely on this officer to help him and watch his back. This officer refused to enter the building with Aiken. He said that a TACT (now known as SWAT) team had been dispatched and was on the way. Aiken begged him to go in and not wait for the TACT team, but he steadfastly refused. To this day, Aiken feels that if this other officer had gone in with him that together they could have saved Officer Hester. He remains bitterly disappointed over this officer's refusal to help. He knew and respected this officer, but after his refusal to help, he had little use for him. This officer remained on the department for only a short period of time after the Shannon Street incident before resigning. However, he did not leave law enforcement altogether, he became an investigator with the state attorney's office. Was he under orders not to go inside? No one knows for certain, but it is doubtful. Whether Aiken and this other officer could have saved Hester remains in doubt, but there is no doubt at all that he certainly would have had a better chance at surviving than he ended up with.

Aiken continued returning fire, but he heard over the radio the subject he was firing at was screaming that if the police did not stop shooting at him he was "going to kill the motherfucker." Aiken ceased fire and finally withdrew from the house out the rear doorway for the last time. The mysterious officer who handed him the shotgun was still nowhere to be seen. Aiken ran back to the front and advised Lt. C. R. Summers that there was an officer down in the house and that he had been shot twice. He also told him that he was out of ammunition. Summer gave him more bullets. Officer Aiken then returned to the rear of the house, aided by another officer, Patrolman Steve Parker. As Parker and Aiken silently made their way around the rear, they could hear a police radio underneath a window. Both officers then witnessed a flash, most likely from another gunshot from inside the house, but oddly, they did not hear it go off. Aiken and Parker then retreated to the corners at the rear of the house and stayed there until finally being relieved by officers from the TACT team hours later. He had entered the house on three different occasions, under fire, in an attempt to rescue Hester and Schwill. Patrolman Aiken showed the courage and dedication to his profession and reflected in the finest traditions of the Memphis Police Department and law enforcement agencies everywhere. Officer Aiken was to receive the second highest award for bravery in the Memphis Police Department, the Medal of Valor, for his actions that cold January night. His actions that evening are still taught at the Memphis Police Academy to new recruits. His level of bravery and tactics utilized is a model that could not have been crafted any better by a single individual even if he had hours to plot out a course of action. He continues to serve the residents of Memphis at the time this book was written although he is due to retire shortly. His departure from the MPD will leave a vacancy few will be qualified to fulfill.

CHAPTER 14

Reserve Officers

Memphis Reserve Officer James Norton had been a police officer for eighteen months in January of 1983. Reserve police officers serve an important function in the MPD. In fact, most departments in the United States use to reserve officers in one form or another to supplement the duties of regular officers. Most reserve officers receive little or no pay for the job they do. Most are strictly volunteers, but their training must meet state standards for law enforcement officers, which is normally the same training full-time police officers receive. The advantage to the city and department is that more cars can be on the street increasing visibility. Also, reserves can work functions normally frowned upon or are difficult to fill by regular officers. Details such as public events, parades, sporting events, concerts, etc., are usually not easy spots to fill as regular officers usually frown upon them. Cities can, and usually do, charge event promoters for the additional strain their events place on police departments. Filling these slots with reserve officers allows the city to recoup any monies set aside for security by these promoters. All reserves must attend the police academy, and they receive much the same training that regular officers must go through. As with the retail establishments, these promoters would prefer seeing uniformed police officers at their functions rather than security officers. Hiring a private security firm is an option many promoters elect to do because it is normally less money than hiring off-duty police officers. However, off-duty officers and uniformed reserves command more respect and attention than security guards in the eyes of the public. Reserve Officer Norton graduated from the Memphis Police Academy in May of 1981. He volunteered to protect and serve, and on the night of January 11, he was patrolling alone in a one-man squad car. He was parked at the time the call went out, talking with another officer, Patrolman Tommy Turner, who was also to distinguish himself at Shannon Street. Norton was not dispatched to the call, but since he was only a short distance away at the time the call went out from dispatch, he responded. He followed Turner, lights and sirens blaring, and arrived on the scene within two minutes. While en route to the scene, Norton heard an officer screaming over the radio for help. This certainly added to the drama that was building rapidly. When he arrived, he immediately ran to the front door where he witnessed a subject in the doorway. This subject was squatting in the doorway holding something in his hand. When he saw the flash and heard the distinctive sound of a round being fired, and in his direction, he pulled his weapon and rapidly fired four rounds at the subject. He then ran to the cover of a car parked in the front of the house. From this vantage point, Norton heard more shots being fired. He then witnessed an officer running from the front porch holding his head in his hands. This turned out to be Officer Tommy Turner who had been struck across the head as he attempted to enter the front door. Within a few minutes, he witnessed another officer, obviously in pain and bleeding from the head, run out the front door. With little regard for his own safety, Officer Norton jumped up out of his position of cover and ran to the officer's side. He guided the officer (Schwill) to the safety of the car he had originally taken cover behind. Schwill was bleeding heavily from his head, but he was conscious and he appeared to be going into shock. Norton radioed for an ambulance while another officer helped Schwill into another patrol car. This patrol car rushed Officer Schwill to the hospital. While this was taking place, Norton could still hear gunshots coming from the house. He saw another officer standing behind the large oak tree in the front yard, a few short feet from the front door. He offered to cover this officer should he want to retreat to the safety behind the car. He refused. Ed Vidulich was not a man to back down from a fight, and he felt that his best chance to help was standing behind the huge oak tree in the front yard. It was on this tree that Sanders had nailed his poster about Mr. Hog.

Shortly thereafter, the TACT team arrived on the scene, and Norton was ordered to assist with securing the perimeter. He remained at this location until he was relieved by an Alpha shift unit. As his shift was ending, he realized that he had violated department policy as he failed to notify his superiors that he had fired his weapon. According to Memphis Police Department policy at the time, whenever an officer discharges his weapon, even accidentally, he must contact the supervisor on duty and advise him of his actions. He is to also draft a report of the incident and be available for an interview with the Internal Affairs Department. Before going home, he contacted an investigator with the violent crimes unit and advised him of his actions on Shannon Street. He was told to contact the security squad to advise them. He went to the north precinct to discuss this with his commanding officer who also directed him to contact the security squad. In his interview with the security squad, he was asked if he thought he had struck any of the suspects when he fired his four rounds. He stated that he did not think he hit anyone when he fired. He was right.

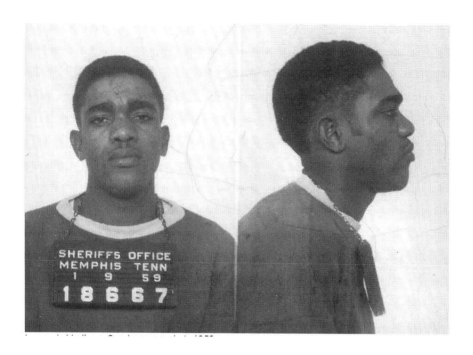

Lindberg Sanders mug shot, 1959

"Wanted For Murder, Mr. Pig" nailed to the tree outside 2239 Shannon St.

Rear of 2239 Shannon St. the day after

Blood splattered front porch. The titles are still there today

Officer's Hester and Schwill's Patrol car

2239 Shannon St. Note the large tree in the small font yard.
Patrolman Ed Vidulich hid behind this tree for hours

Tires flattened by the police to prevent escape attempts

Round bed where one hostage taker was killed. Note handgun on the edge

Investigators gather outside the morning after

Patrolman's leather jacket found on the sofa inside the house

Chaotic scene inside the rear of the house where Officer Russ
Aiken repeatedly entered attempting to rescue the officers.

Bloody scene inside the living room. Note MPD radio.
The blood is most likely officer Ray Schwills.

CHAPTER 15

Heroes

By this time, additional officers arrived on the scene, and Patrolman Russ Aiken was ordered not to make any more attempts at rescue. Bitter and frustrated at not being able to rescue Hester and at being ordered to stand down, Aiken reluctantly took up a position around the perimeter of the property. The scene was unfolding into a hostage scenario, and negotiators were being called to the scene to attempt to resolve the situation peacefully. No doubt Aiken's actions helped save the life of Officer Schwill. The gunfire that erupted from the rear of the house created the diversion Schwill needed to make his break to safety. No less a hero in this endeavor is Officer Turner who was entering the building through the front while Aiken was breaching the rear of the house. Turner never had the chance to fire his weapon, although he did try, as he was ambushed as soon as he entered the front door knocking his weapon out of commission. The subjects saw and heard him coming, and they were prepared. Aiken took the subjects in the rear by surprise. Working with uncoordinated coordination and a team, Aiken and Turner saved a life that cold evening in January of 1983. They thought little of their own safety; the only thing on their mind was that another officer needed help, and they were going to give it. If the roles were reversed and it was them inside that house, there was no doubt in their minds that Schwill and Hester would have done the same for them. They had successfully enabled Officer Schwill to escape; now it was time to rescue the second officer inside. All they needed was a plan. Aiken felt that he could pull off a rescue; all he needed was a little help. The officer he pleaded with in the rear of the house would not help him, but surely there was someone that would. Enough commanders were now on the scene, and surely, they were putting together a plan to get inside. Aiken wanted nothing more than to be a part of the overall rescue attempt. He knew the inside layout of the house better than anyone else around. What better man to use than Officer Russ Aiken? He would never be given the chance, and Officer Bobby Hester would meet a fate that would leave officers disgusted and demoralized. However, events were about to spiral out of control, and the result would be a tragedy the likes that Memphis had never seen before. Both had done all that they could, and now it was up to the hostage negotiators to try and bring this to a peaceful conclusion. Officer Turner had been injured and was being sent home after receiving numerous stitches and returning to Shannon Street. Officer Aiken had dodged death and injury with his repeated assaults in the rear of the building. He remained at his position throughout the night. He wasn't going to give up hope that he could be involved in the rescue.

CHAPTER 16

Ed Vidulich

Meanwhile, at the front of the house, the situation was becoming desperate. As officers arrived, they took cover wherever they could find it. When Officer Ed Vidulich and his partner William Downen arrived on the scene, Vidulich took cover behind an enormous oak tree in the front yard placing him no more than six to eight feet from the front door. He was in perfect position to cover the entry of Officer Turner. This position gave him a better view of the entire front house than anyone. His partner took cover behind a squad car parked on the street in front of the house, probably the unit Schwill and Hester were using that night. There were shots being fired into the house by officers, and Vidulich was screaming for them to hold their fire as he knew there were Memphis police officers still inside the residence. He knew that Officers Schwill and Hester were trapped inside the house and that other officers were attempting to gain entry both in the front and also the rear. It is not certain if he knew about Officer Aiken's attempts at rescue in the rear, but most likely, he saw Aiken running toward the back, and he was worried that he would be hurt by the seemingly random shots being fired at the home. He did not want anyone hurt by friendly fire. No one had yet taken control of the situation, and he saw many officers not working together as a unit. Someone had to take control and Vidulich was prepared to do so. His actions most likely prevented a lot of out-of-control fire from the arriving officers. It was dark inside the house, and all the smoke was not helping at all. In spite of his efforts, shots still continued to ring out. Vidulich witnessed Schwill escape out the front door and his partner got him to the cover of the squad car. Finally, it became quiet around the property after Schwill made his escape. There was screaming coming from inside the property, but while everyone on the scene heard it, most could not identify the source. Officer Hester was yelling for help and wanted the department to rescue him. He knew that help had arrived and had to be thinking that rescue was going to happen momentarily. Many officers on the scene could hear him screaming periodically. Lindberg Sanders had recovered Hester's radio and was using it to yell at the police. In the background, all the officers on duty that night could hear the plaintive cries of Bobby Hester. None would ever be able to forget that night. Most would hear those screams over and over in their nightmares. Ed Vidulich was to stay behind that tree for hours, tantalizingly close to the front door, but powerless to get inside to rescue the hostaged officer. He was eventually relieved when the Memphis TACT unit arrived on scene. He was happy to see the arrival of the TACT team. It seemed as though it had taken them forever to get there, but now that they were on the scene, it wouldn't be long before the rescue attempt would finally begin. Russ Aiken, still in position at the rear of the property watching the back door, also heard the TACT team arrive. He silently breathed a sigh of intense relief. Now finally, it wouldn't be long before they rescue would begin. He believed that a direct assault, with some sort of diversion, would bring this to a close quickly. He was right about that, but if he wanted a quick rescue attempt, it was not going to be here. Little did he know that politicians were beginning to become aware of Shannon Street. Had he known that, he would have known that things would turn out badly.

CHAPTER 17

St. Jude Children's Hospital

The Memphis Police Department had some recent experience in hostage taking. Less than a year earlier, a disgruntled father who had lost his only child to cancer at St. Jude Children's Hospital calmly arrived at the reception area early one morning. He pulled a gun from a bag he was carrying and told the receptionist to page certain hospital staff members. After they arrived, the gunman, forty-year-old Jean Claude Goulet, a Canadian citizen living in Louisiana, took them hostage and moved them into a small room off the receptionist area. Goulet held the people captive because he wanted the world to know what happened to his six-year-old son. He demanded that a cure be found for the leukemia that took the life of his only child. The Memphis Police Department brought negotiators to the scene and immediately began talking to him. He produced a number of demands, most notably an eight-page statement he had written that he wanted broadcasted over a local radio station. This demand was granted and WMC radio in Memphis broadcast the message. Goulet was given a portable radio and was able to listen to the broadcast. After it ended, he was suspicious and did not believe that it was the same message he had written. He then demanded that it be replayed on every radio station in Memphis. Police officials went to the media representatives and asked that they play the tape. WMC, along with a few other stations, agreed. Then realizing they had a powerful story, the stations continued playing the recording over and over, which upset police officials on the scene. They were worried that the continuous replaying of the tape would make it appear that Goulet was some kind of hero and that he was being portrayed as a victim. Goulet had agreed to release one of the hostages once the tape had been played. Afterward, he refused. This infuriated negotiators on the scene, and they now knew that they were dealing with someone they could not trust. Hostage negotiations are built on trust between the police and the suspect. When a suspect agrees to do something and fails to do so, experienced hostage negotiators know they are dealing with a situation that could get ugly and quickly. Extra precautions are taken, and the climate becomes far tenser for all.

Goulet was rambling over the phone, and concern grew internally over the safety of the hostages. As the hours dragged on, food was brought to the scene, and one of the hostages, Dr. George Marten, sixty-four, a psychiatrist, was released. Goulet had lived up to his word to release a hostage once food was delivered. Things seemed to be going as planned as far as the department was concerned. Now three hostages remained: Jo Cummins, a psychological examiner; Dr. Paul Bowman, a pediatrician and member of the leukemia research team; and Jean Cox, a staff nurse. Goulet was familiar with all four of the original hostages and called them by name. Obviously, he had planned this in great detail. It had been over a year since the death of his son, so he had plenty of time to plan his assault. He was going to make the world know that he was cheated by the death of his son. St. Jude Children's Hospital was started by the entertainer Danny Thomas. His daughter Marlo Thomas is now the spokesperson for many hospital fund-raisers. The institution is known throughout the world as one of the leaders in the treatment of children's diseases. The work they do produces miracles, and if the children's family cannot afford treatment, it is given without hesitation. There are even rooms provided for families from out of town to use while their child is undergoing treatment. These rooms are funded entirely by donations, and residents are allowed to stay there at no charge to them. The environment at this lodging is family oriented. The families get to stay there with other families facing similar hardships. It permits the families to bond together, and they all react positively toward one another. Many former residents have praised the Ronald McDonald House and felt blessed to be allowed to stay there. As many of the children who are patients at the hospital require extended treatments, not having to worry about lodging costs allow the patients to have loved ones nearby all the time. This certainly can aid in their recuperation. And the family does not have the cost burden to worry about.

CHAPTER 18

Rescue at St. Jude

As negotiators continued trying to work to free the hostages and bring the incident to a peaceful ending, time was working against a successful resolution. Meetings were held at the highest levels of the police department. It was decided that they could wait no longer to attempt a rescue of the hostages and that they had to move at the first opportunity. TACT team members formulated a plan to gain entry to the room. It would be the ultimate assault, and they had trained for scenarios similar to this one many times. They would send officers to flank the only entryway into the room the hostages were being held captive. Another officer was to gain entry through a duct in the ceiling. This officer had to drag himself through a narrow tunnel of soft aluminum to get into position. He was in a very vulnerable position as he was in a very exposed location. One small noise could erupt in gunfire, and the thin aluminum offered little protection. As the officers were being deployed, Goulet heard a noise in the ceiling and became suspicious. If he had fired his weapon at the noise, the officer would be trapped and injured and perhaps killed. Sgt. Jim Kellum was the officer in the duct work, and he was in big trouble. Goulet dragged a table over to a vent in the ceiling. He climbed on top and shoved the grate aside. Kellum heard the grate moving and was powerless to do anything. He could not get to his weapon as there was not enough room to maneuver. He prayed to become invisible, but he expected gunfire to erupt at any moment. As Goulet was looking into the vent, one of the hostages, Dr. Bowman, saw his chance to act. He grabbed at Goulet's legs while he was standing on top of the table. Goulet fell and landed on top of Bowman.

Kellum heard the noise and couldn't figure out what was going on. He thought maybe he had not been seen, but felt this would have taken a miracle. One of the other hostages screamed, which alerted TACT team members who immediately burst into the room. Seeing Bowman and Goulet locked in a life or death struggle, officers fired four rounds, and Goulet died at the scene. No one else was seriously injured in the incident, although Dr. Bowman did suffer a minor shoulder injury during the struggle. The hostages all stated that the officers had no choice and that they were convinced that Goulet was not going to surrender peaceably. They all felt that he was going to drag the situation out as long as he could so that the publicity surrounding the event would be maximized. Suicide by cop was not a term used in 1982, but it seemed to all the hostages that this could have been his ultimate goal. The fact that officers were able to bring the situation to a conclusion without any of the hostages being harmed reflected positively on the department and its personnel.

CHAPTER 19

Negotiations with Sanders

With this incident still fresh in the minds of police officials, they were determined to end the Shannon Street confrontation peacefully. Some of the same people that handled the negotiations at St. Jude would be on the scene at Shannon Street. While both incidents were obvious hostage situations with potentially dire consequences, Shannon Street had little in common with the incident at St. Jude's Children's Hospital. At St. Jude's, the perpetrator was in contact with police officials. He was making demands, albeit sometimes irrational ones, but the line of communication was kept open. Normally, experts in negotiating feel that as long as they keep the subject talking, they have a much better chance at a peaceful conclusion. Nothing concerns negotiators more than a subject that refuses to talk or negotiate. Also, no one was being physically tortured by Goulet. While uncomfortable, there was no physical abuse, but the effects of the mental abuse cannot be ignored.

As events unfurled at Shannon Street, officers on the scene could hear Officer Hester being beaten. Sanders often refused to talk to police negotiators over the phone. He communicated with them via the police radio that he had taken from Hester. When Hester was pleading for his life and begging police to rescue him, Sanders would push the Talk button on the police radio. Every officer on the scene could hear his plaintive cries. In fact, officers throughout the city could hear the transmissions. Anyone with a scanner tuned into the correct frequency could also hear everything. The Memphis Police Department had the small frame home surrounded. The MPD TACT team arrived on the scene and took over positions occupied by regular patrol officers who had been the first to respond to the cries for help. They had the home completely surrounded. Snipers were positioned around the home including on the rooftop of the elementary school directly across the street from the house on Shannon Avenue. That school still stands today and looks much like it did back in January of 1983. A temporary command post was set up in one of the rooms in the school. Various high-ranking police officials were arriving on the scene throughout the night. Some political leaders also took the occasion to visit the scene and offer their help. The police director arrived. He was a lifelong member of the Memphis Police Department, but he had only been in this position for a few short months. Director John Holt had joined the Memphis Police Department in September of 1952. Holt had been with the MPD for over thirty years and had held many different positions within the department. On January 13, 1983, he was thrown into a situation that was impossible to prepare for. Officers were continuously trained in hostage situations, but never with another officer being held as the hostage. The closest any department had ever come to a similar situation had occurred in Los Angeles. This incident involved a pair of officers who, during a routine traffic stop, ended up being taken hostage by a couple of small-time thugs. This story was chronicled in the brilliant book *The Onion Field* by former Los Angeles Police Officer Joseph Wambaugh. The incident chronicled in *The Onion Field* led to a policy change in virtually every police department in America. The two police officers involved in *The Onion Field* decided to pull over a car that looked suspicious. They had no idea that the two occupants of the car had recently committed an armed robbery. During the stop, one of the occupants got out of the car on the passenger side and pulled a gun on the officer approaching. He ordered the other officer to drop his weapon, which he ultimately did. Both cops were taken hostage and driven to an isolated area in Southern California that was an actual onion field. The cops were forced to the side of the road in the pitch-black darkness. The first officer was executed with a bullet to the back of his head. The other officer jumped up and ran into the field. The gunmen searched frantically for him, but they couldn't find him in the dark. The gunmen were eventually caught and prosecuted. Both were sentenced to death. The surviving officer suffered for years and was eventually forced to quit the department. This was long before agencies recognized the stress involved in law enforcement. He was never given counseling, and he suffered miserably from survivor's guilt. Since the onion field incident, police departments regularly trained their officers never to surrender their weapons. But no one had envisioned a scenario like the one unfolding in Memphis this night. The decision was made to attempt to negotiate the release of Officer Hester. Attempts to contact the house went unanswered. When Sanders finally answered the phone, he was incoherent and rambling. He did tell the negotiators that he wanted to talk to a local radio disc jockey. It was the only demand he made in thirty hours of on-again, off-again negotiations. He had informed the officers that he had a gun held against the head of officer Hester and that if any attempt was made to get inside the house, he was going to pull the trigger and "blow his motherfuckin' head off." He had mentioned that the reason he wanted to talk with the disc jockey was so that he could murder the officer live on the air for all to hear. As was mentioned previously, the disc jockey held some sort of attraction to Sanders. He would listen to his radio program from the time he signed on until it was over. The request was denied, although the DJ was on the scene for a period of time. He offered to do anything he could to help resolve the crisis. This should have alerted the negotiators that the chances of a peaceful resolution were not good.

CHAPTER 20

Family Brought In

The officers did bring Sanders's wife to the scene in an attempt to get him to give up, but she was powerless to help. His daughter also was unable to get through to him. He refused to talk to either of them, even after repeated attempts by the negotiators. Every single attempt to get through to Sanders failed. The even talked with neighbors who they felt might be close enough to the subject, but none of them were of any use whatsoever. They tried, but Sanders refused to respond to any of them.

The staff was in a real quandary with the life of a police officer at stake. The question that was going through the minds of many at the scene was what if it was a citizen being held hostage and not a police officer? Would the response by the police director in command of the scene been any different? No one can answer that question and it lingers to this day. Is the life of a police officer worth any more or less than anyone else's? In the St. Jude's Children's Hospital incident the year before, the TACT team was given permission to secure the release of the hostages when attempts at negotiations failed quickly. And these hostages were not being tortured like Officer Hester was. The department was in a real quandary. Not only had Director Holt been a relative newcomer to the job, the mayor of Memphis had only himself recently been elected to the position. He was elected in a special election to fulfill the remaining term of former Mayor Wyeth Chandler who had resigned to take an appointment to the state court. The police director, John Holt, was a seasoned veteran of law enforcement. He knew procedures and policy. There could not have been a more talented, experienced commander on the scene than John Holt. The city's new mayor, Dick Hackett, was white, and as he had about a year left to serve before he was up for re-election, he was sensitive to the black community. He had no experience in law enforcement, and he was the one in command. The fact that blacks had taken white officers hostage only made Hackett more resolved to end the incident peaceably. He did not want race to become an issue, but it seems that race always clouds issues in Memphis, even to this day, as in many other cities across the country.

CHAPTER 21

No Demands

Officers could hear Hester as Sanders periodically keyed the microphone, screaming as he was being beaten. However, the battery in Hester's radio began to fail. Sanders had refused to talk to negotiators over the telephone, and officers repeatedly had told Sanders that the battery was going to be worn out soon. They wanted him to use the phone instead, but he again refused. They even made replacement radio batteries available to him, but they were never used. They were doing everything they could, but nothing seemed to be working as it should.

They soon knew they were dealing with an irrational subject in Lindberg Sanders. They had been told by some of the neighbors that Sanders was an outdoorsman and that there were many weapons in the home. All the draperies had been pulled closed, and it was impossible for them to see inside. At some point, the police had the power to the house cut off. They were not certain exactly how many men were inside the home. They had a layout of the home, but it was impossible for them to know where everyone was located. They knew there were at least five additional subjects, probably more, and not knowing where all of them were made any rescue attempt a gamble. Also, not knowing how many weapons were in the home made the risk even greater. The decision was made to continue the attempts at negotiations to resolve the standoff. This, in spite of the fact that there were no demands made by Sanders, except for his desire to speak with the disc jockey. The police were hopeful that he would come to his senses and eventually surrender. The police could still hear Hester being beaten, but the decision to attempt a rescue was delayed until more intelligence could be gathered. A police dispatcher had initially been ordered to call the house. He succeeded in getting Sanders on the phone, and he repeatedly asked about the condition of the hostage. Every time he asked, the officers listening in to the radio could hear Sanders hit Officer Hester. Finally, a staff officer had to contact the dispatcher and tell him to stop asking about the condition of Officer Hester.

Sanders continued his harangue against the police. He had earlier told his psychiatrist that the Memphis Police Department had killed him a few years before and that God had brought him back to life for a purpose. He also complained to this doctor that he had been beaten by a white motorcycle gang. He had told his followers that the world was going to end in a few days. Sanders believed that pork was the work of the devil. There was a poster tacked up to the huge oak tree in the front of Sanders's home that showed a pig in the center with the words "Wanted for Murder" written underneath it. It was under this poster, Patrolman Ed Vidulich (who was destined to be brutally murdered in his own home a number of years later) stood for hours until he was finally relieved when the TACT team showed up. Vidulich was less than six feet from the main entrance in the front of the house, and he could hear Hester's pleadings. It was the most horrific experience in the long career of this fine officer. Those cries for help would haunt him for the rest of his life.

CHAPTER 22

Listening Devices

Meanwhile, police on the scene had requested that a microphone be placed inside the home in order to listen in on the people inside. A call went out to headquarters to secure this equipment, which was relatively new at the time. In the meantime, one of the officers on the scene approached a television reporter from Atlanta and asked him if he had a microphone. The reporter went to the trunk of his car and produced one that he was welcome to use. He and his partner cautiously approached the house and succeeded in placing the microphone between the floorboards. Meanwhile, the microphone arrived a few hours later from headquarters, and two other officers were able to crawl up to one of the outside walls of the home. In this wall was a window that had been broken out sometime during the initial assault. The officers were able to place the microphone through the broken glass. Sergeant Jim Kellum crept up to the side of the house to place the microphone through the window. He was certain that at any minute gunfire would erupt from behind the curtain and that he would be trapped between the two buildings with nowhere to go. Now the police had some genuine intelligence gathering capability. The microphones gave the police an advantage in that they were able to listen in. Unfortunately, hours passed with no dialogue coming from inside the house. Many on the scene wondered if everyone had gone to sleep. Listening devices back in 1983 were primitive when compared to what is available today. Another problem that presented itself was linking the listening devices together. The devices installed on Shannon Street helped, but there was only a single set of headphones, and only one officer could hear what was taking place inside. This officer was not in direct communication with the hostage negotiators. He was in a home right next door to the house where Hester was being held hostage. The hostage negotiators were located at the command post in the school across the street. He could hear the negotiators attempting to speak with Sanders, and he could hear his replies. However, since the battery eventually failed on the radio Sanders was using, the negotiators believed that he was refusing to negotiate. Since they could not hear any response coming from inside the home, they truly did not know what to expect. The officer with the headset could hear everything. Sanders was responding to the negotiators, but since the battery was gone, they failed to hear him. The officer on the headphones could hear very well, and he was confused when a question was asked of Sanders and he responded, but the hostage negotiators failed to respond. Only later did this officer, Sgt. Jim Kellum, realize that he was the only one that could hear Sanders. Every one of Sanders's responses was irrational, and it was obvious that he was out of control. Kellum could not figure out at the time why the negotiators were saying that Sanders would not respond. One question the negotiators had asked was about the condition of Officer Hester. Sanders's response was that the "police wanted him to cooperate, but that all pigs must die, all pigs were liars." He also stated that "all this shit started when the pigs accused him of stealing a purse." He then stated, "The pigs wanted me to cooperate, and I'll cooperate by giving them back something they want, but they aren't going to like the condition it's in." Kellum then listened as Sanders now directed his attention to someone inside the house, Patrolman Bobby Hester. He told him, "Yeah, motherfucker, you're bleeding, but I'm bleeding too." Sanders then said, "You're gonna die, and all the pigs around this house are going to die too." Sanders then apparently went into another room because Kellum could no longer make out what he was saying. Sergeant Kellum stated that there was no audible response from anyone inside the house to the comments made by Sanders. He was still baffled as to why the negotiators were not responding to Sanders and his comments. He assumed that since he could clearly hear what was being said, that they could too. Regrettably, this was not the case. Eventually, Kellum tried to word to get to the command post about his microphone being active, but by the time he realized what the problem was, it was too late to make a difference.

The officers, again using the police radio to communicate with Sanders, again asked him to use the telephone. They were afraid that the battery on the radio would give out soon cutting off all communications, which had already happened. Sanders would periodically answer the phone, but would go back to the radio. He didn't seem to care to listen to anything the negotiators were saying, he simply wanted the people listening over the police radio to hear what was going on inside the home. He wanted all the officers to hear what he was doing to Hester. All attempts at negotiations had failed, but still, they held out hope that Sanders would give up. Officers on the scene could sometimes hear, through the thin walls of the structure, Officer Hester moaning and in obvious pain. They were frustrated and upset that the longer they waited and did nothing, the worse it looked for Hester. There were some officers who were tempted to affect a rescue on their own. All wanted to put an end to the situation and rescue the officer.

Officers said later they had placed themselves in Hester's position as a hostage in order to better determine what they would want done if it had been them. Every officer said they would want and expect their brother officers to attempt a rescue and let the chips fall where they may. No one would want to suffer through what Officer Hester was forced to endure. He was treated like an animal.

CHAPTER 23

The Thin Blue Line

Police officers are a rare and unique breed. The "thin blue line" as officers commonly refer to their profession consists of men and women who have sworn to "serve and protect."

To most officers, this is more than simply words written on the outside of police cars. It is a creed that they live by. Most get into law enforcement for the simple reason that it a profession whereby they can truly make a difference. One person can influence the lives of countless individuals, and the satisfaction one gets from turning lives around is a reward that no amount of money can ever replace. And they certainly don't do it for the money. Departments all across the country pay teachers, administrators, trash collectors, bus drivers, and especially bureaucrats more money than police officers. Whenever municipalities get into financial trouble, the local politicians talk about the eventual cuts in "essential services" like police and firefighting. Seldom, if ever, do you hear about cuts in their own staffs. This is intentional as they seem to want to punish their constituents for the shortfalls in the budget that are usually because of their own mismanagement. The best way to do this is to threaten to cut back the number of police officers and firemen on the street. These dimwitted politicians think that if the public believes that they are going to become less safe, then they will come around and agree to pay higher taxes. Of course, cutbacks can be made in other areas within the usually bloated bureaucracy, but this almost never happens. Rarely are these politicians called to task over these threats. It simply does not occur. The media usually fails to hold these people accountable for their actions.

The report revenue shortfalls, but rarely dig deeper into where the money went. That would be where the real story should be.

Certainly there are officers who take the job for other reasons than a simple wish to help. However, it is the officers who have the desire to leave their footprint on society that make up the nucleus of a good department. All good cops are fully committed men and women. You have to be in order to thrive in a world where you are always seeing people at their absolute worst. Whether as a victim of a crime, in an automobile crash, or being given a ticket, cops see people at some of the worst times of their lives. They rarely get to interface with them when things are good. The camaraderie inherent within police departments is significant. The members may bicker about petty things, but like in a family, if anyone from the outside criticizes an individual member, they close ranks quickly and will defend that person passionately. On the street, they are continuously watching out for each other. When an officer puts out a call for assistance, cops from all over the city will rush to his aid.

CHAPTER 24

Hours Drag On

Hours dragged on with little or no contact with the hostage takers. For the cops on the scene, the adrenaline rush had long since worn off and fatigue now became the enemy. There had been numerous shift changes since this the start of the assault. Alpha shift was relieved by Bravo shift and Bravo by Charlie shift. Fresh officers were on the scene always, but still, fatigue would set in, along with frustration and anger. The cops were wondering what was happening. Was everyone simply asleep? Earlier, some officers could hear banging noises coming from somewhere inside the house. With Sanders's background in construction, he had plenty of tools and equipment lying around. The general feeling was that barricades were being built within the interior of the home. If this was true, then the prospects for a peaceful conclusion were pretty bleak. What kinds of barricades were being constructed? The police had no way of knowing because they could not see into the structure. As quickly as the sounds of construction started, they stopped. Whatever was being done inside the house was completed. Now the MPD had another problem to contend with. For one, they still had no idea just how many men were inside. They also had no idea how many weapons they had. They knew the two officers' handguns were taken by the suspects, but they did not know what other types of guns or weapons they had. They had been warned earlier that Sanders was an avid hunter and fisherman, so they assumed he had a number of different guns inside. Sanders's wife had not lived in the home for quite a while, so she had no idea what he may have had inside. The TACT team had been on the scene for hours, and they had drawn up a number of different plans to assault the building. Many different ideas were discussed, reviewed, and then discarded as the scenario was changing. An assault during daylight hours constitutes different problems than an assault under the cover of darkness. The TACT team had to plan for many different contingencies. There was increasing pressure to bring this to a conclusion, but politics also played a role. The mayor wanted every effort geared toward a peaceful resolution. He did not want an assault made until every possible avenue for a peaceful resolution was explored. He did make an appearance at the command post, but did not spend much time there. He gave his orders and left. It was up to Director Holt and the MPD to end the conflict without further incident. Hackett was playing politics while an officer who had sworn to protect and serve the city and the mayor was being brutally beaten. The murder of Officer Bobby Hester must have plagued Mayor Dick Hackett the rest of his life.

CHAPTER 25

Decision Time

It had been hours since anyone had heard anything from Officer Hester. The microphones planted earlier had not provided any useful information either. It was pretty quiet inside and had been for a number of hours. Had everyone simply gone to sleep? The hostage negotiators were still trying to establish contact with the people inside, but because they had not been linked with people manning the hidden microphones, they were not aware of anyone inside responding to their attempts in communicating. In fact, when they would use the bullhorn, there would be occasional answers, but the negotiators could not hear them. The microphones picked up some of the answers, and the officer with the headset could not understand why the negotiators were not responding back when answered. He naturally assumed that they (the negotiators) could hear the people inside responding. The responses were incoherent and at the same time threatening. Once, when the negotiators on the bullhorn inquired about the health of the officer, Sanders responded by stating that "they weren't going to like the shape he's in when you get him back." This response was never heard by the negotiators, but the officer manning the headphones heard it clearly and was baffled by the lack of response by the negotiators.

The head of the police officers union, Ray Maples, had remained on the scene throughout its entirety. He was one of those who were thinking about assaulting the house on his own. He was frustrated and angry that nothing had been done. He knew the director, John Holt, and always had the utmost respect for him. He felt that Holt was more than sympathetic to the plight of the average

Memphis police officer. Years later, Maples would tell me that he thought John Holt was the finest police director he had ever worked with. In fact, the current Memphis Police Department Academy is named after John Holt. As with any union-versus-management scenario, there can be mistrust of the main parties involved. The Memphis Police Association did not become a recognized union by the city until 1973. Grudgingly, the politicians realized that the time had come for recognition. Ray Maples was elected the head of the union in 1979. He was to hold that position for many years, up until shortly before his retirement. He was a scrappy fighter who seemed to be constantly battling the politicians and administrative officials within the department. He was successful in securing higher wages and better working conditions for his members. He was constantly at odds with Director Holt. But this did not impact his attitude toward the director personally. He had known Holt before he became the union president and always respected him as a police officer. He knew Holt would do anything in his power to rescue Officer Hester.

But Maples was not aware of everything that was taking place at the command post on Shannon Street; all he knew was that he could hear a brother officer in obvious pain, and everyone there wanted to go in and put an end to his suffering. He was confused by what he perceived as a lack of urgency on the part of the command staff. All the officers wanted to go in immediately to rescue Hester, but nothing along those lines seemed to be happening. No planning could be seen by Maples, no briefings were taking place, nothing at all was being done in his eyes. It seemed to him that everyone was content to continue the frustrating job of negotiating. After hours and hours of negotiations, things were no different than they had been when he first arrived on the scene. He states in no uncertain terms, that he personally approached the director and gave him an ultimatum: that if an assault was not undertaken within the next sixty minutes, he was going to get union members who were ready, willing, and able to secure Hester's rescue. This was no idle threat. Maples had the backing of most of all the officers on the scene. They knew him and trusted him. They were frustrated and angry with the manner in which the situation had been handled so far, and there is no doubt that had Holt failed to respond to this demand, that Maples would have carried out on his promise. Holt was every bit as frustrated and angry as the rest of the officers there. He wanted Hester out of there and in a hospital. His hands were tied as he had to take orders from the politicians. Maples's demand most likely presented him with the option he needed. That is, he now was forced to take action. Negotiations had failed miserably, and it was time to end this situation another way. A direct assault was the only option remaining. He ordered the TACT team to saddle up because they were going in.

Afterward, Maples would blast the handling of the situation in the press. He was frustrated and angry, and a reporter happened to be near and asked him all the right questions. Maples did not hold back when reporters quizzed him about Shannon Street. He was angry, frustrated, exhausted, and crushed when confronted with the death of one of his men, so he let loose with this reporter. Later, he realized that this was not the way to do things. The department was not happy with his comments to the press. Pressure was put on Maples to retract his story, which he eventually succumbed to. He apologized to the press and said that he had spoken in the heat of the moment and that his words had been taken out of context. He also stated that he was simply Monday-morning quarterbacking. But it did not quell the passion inside Ray Maples. He demanded that a policy be written allowing the individual officer taken hostage to have a say in whether or not he wanted the troops sent in to save him. He was quoted in the *Memphis Press Scimitar* newspaper saying, "This whole thing confirms my belief that an officer should be able to choose his own destiny in that kind of situation, it's not right to let a policeman simply be tortured to death."

"We should have a written policy," Maples is quoted as saying, "that will tell every police officer exactly what will happen if he gets in that situation. If I was Hester I would have called for the TACT unit to come in." At one point during the over-thirty-hours siege, Hester did plead with his fellow officers to attempt a rescue. The implication of Hester's statement, however, was that he had endured such pain that he preferred a quick death. The department assigned this task to a committee made up of officers and staff from throughout the department.

Holt could have ordered him (Maples) off the site and that would have been the end of it. But Holt did no such thing. No doubt he was having some of the same concerns that Maples had. He called another officer over that he respected. He asked this officer what his opinion was. He knew that Sergeant Jim Kellum had been listening in on all the negotiations. Kellum had been the one monitoring the headsets that were linked to the microphones that had been hidden inside. Kellum had heard all the threats and rants that had come from inside for hours, and he knew that the time was right for an assault. He stated his opinion that entry should be made as quickly as possible to try and save Hester. Holt had been getting mounting pressure from all sides for hours. The rank and file had been pressing for an assault, and the politicians had been pressing for a peaceful, nonviolent resolution. Holt considered the advice and quickly agreed, and the decision all those on the scene had been awaiting for many hours had finally been made. Kellum had not heard anything from Hester in a long time. The comments he had heard from Sanders about "not liking the shape he's in" had sent a shiver down his spine. Deep down, he feared that Officer Hester was already dead. Twenty-five years after Shannon Street, Kellum still suffers from flashbacks of that night. It was the only incident in his entire thirty-plus-year career that troubles him to this day. Sergeant Kellum was not a desk officer. He had been in thick of many different dangerous situations over the years. A few years after Shannon Street, he was awarded the coveted Medal of Valor award for his actions during another hostage situation that involved a local biker gang in which Kellum was fired upon repeatedly. Sergeant Kellum was a man that Director Holt knew well and respected. If Kellum thought it was time to begin the assault, then Holt knew what he had to do.

A new attitude permeated throughout the command post. They were finally going to go in and rescue Officer Hester. After more than twenty-nine hours of listening to threats, screaming, and nothing, the orders were given, commands made, and assault teams were prepped.

CHAPTER 26

Assault Preparations

The TACT team had been on the scene quickly after the initial call went out. The team stood by on high alert while decisions and plans were evaluated. As the hours dragged on, time had taken its toll on the team. They had stood around for hours, and they needed to be relieved. A tired, dispirited assault team would not be what was needed. So the call went out for another team to relieve the original squad on the scene. This second team, it was decided, would be the one to make the initial entry if and when the time came. They were still fresh, and it was only logical that they would make the assault. The commanders huddled together to begin preparations. Ideas were discussed, evaluated, and digested. The power had been turned off to the house hours before in an attempt to get Sanders to the negotiating table. However, the water was left on. No one thought to turn it off. Having water available could help the occupants of the house should tear gas be used. It was also thought that Sanders might have gas masks inside the home, although this was later determined to be false. It was eventually decided that tear gas would be used along with flash bang grenades. Flash bangs are now in common use in police departments throughout the world, but in 1983, they were relatively new commodities. It was decided that a team of six TACT officers would make the initial assault. There was much discussion about which officers would be on the team. One officer, who was originally named to the team, was told by one of his superiors to refuse the assignment. Naturally, he wanted to be on the team to rescue Hester, so he refused but was then threatened with dire consequences if he did allow the other officer to take his place on the team.

Refusing would have meant that his career as a Memphis police officer and member of the elite TACT unit was over. He had no choice, so he told the team leader that he was too ill to participate and he was excused. His superior was then named to replace him. The six officers selected were the following:

Officer R. O. Watson
Officer C. R. Summers
Officer Ken McNair
Officer H. A. Ray
Officer Dave Hubbard
Officer Don Rutherford

It was decided that three officers would carry standard-issue police shotguns and that the other three would carry the M16 military assault rifle. A couple of the men selected had had previous military training and had served in Vietnam. The men began their preparations for the assault. They used duct tape to secure small flashlights to the ends of their weapons. They went over the plans of the house. Assignments were given to the officers. Each officer ran the plans over in his head. They had to get this right. No mistakes on this one. The life of a police officer was at stake. They had no idea whether or not Bobby Hester was alive or dead, but they were working under the assumption that he was still alive. They checked and rechecked weapons, vests, and all other accessories they might need when the assault began. They wanted a perfect entry. It was dark inside the home as the power had been turned off hours before. There would be a backup team of TACT officers that would be responsible for discharging the flash bang grenades and the tear gas. The timing between this backup team and the initial assault team had to be precise. The element of surprise required that there be an accurate timetable between all the tactical teams. The backup team would receive a coded "blue" message that would indicate that the assault was about to begin. Once they received this message, they would then be responsible in initiating the assault by first shooting tear gas into the structure followed by the flash bangs. Different members would be shooting the flash bangs and tear gas. Coordination was critical. Once the building was secure, it would be the responsibility of the backup team to assist and sweep the premises.

The plan was to create a diversion in the rear of the house and then make entry right through the front door. The TACT team had secured plans of the inside of the house, and the planted microphones gave them some much needed intel, so they had a pretty good idea of where Officer Hester was being held. They also thought they knew where most of the hostage takers were located. The biggest unknown was that over the years there had been extensive remodeling done by Sanders all through the house. Added to this was the noise heard earlier with the hammer and nails. They were not certain what that was all about, but they suspected that barricades had been constructed. There were other unknowns the officers had to contend with that were serious. Intelligence gathering is the key to successful planning, and in this case, they had little to go on except for whatever the microphones provided. Officer Schwill was in surgery and in no position to provide any details. They were not even certain how many people were inside the house. Estimates ranged from as few as two or three to as many as six to ten. They also had no idea what kind of weapons they would encounter once they gained entry. They knew that both of the officers' handguns had been taken away from Hester and Schwill. Neighbors had advised that Sanders and his sons were avid hunters and outdoorsmen, and they had no reason to doubt that there were many different weapons inside. There had also been reports from the first officers arriving on the scene that they had encountered gunfire from inside the house from a number of different calibers of weapons. They suspected that regardless of however many men were still inside that all of them would be armed. They were preparing for the worst, but silently praying for a safe outcome for everyone. They had no desire to do anything more than rescue their brother officer, who they silently prayed was still alive. That was their mission, and they were well trained and well prepared. The TACT team was made up of the best of the best that Memphis law enforcement had to offer. The trained continuously and were at the very top of their game. They were as prepared as they could possibly be. The initial assault team was comprised of six outstanding officers. There would be a backup or secondary assault team of an additional six highly trained and motivated officers. It would be their responsibility to fire the initial rounds of tear gas and concussion grenades into the structure in order to cover the entry on the primary team. Once entry was made, after the secondary team had fired the tear gas and concussion grenades, the secondary team would then take up positions around the house and act as backup if, and when, they were called upon by the initial entry team.

CHAPTER 27

The Rescue Begins

It was time to decide on a plan. The decision had finally been made to rescue Officer Hester and bring this tragedy to an end. After hours and hours of indecision, it was time to go. The final plan decided upon was that there would be two assault teams involved. Assault Team 1 would be led by a seasoned veteran officer, K. K. McNair. Preparatory to the A Team 1 initiating the entry, a barrage of tear gas and concussion grenades would be launched throughout the house in order to cover the four primary and two backup officers' entry. It would be the responsibility of A Team 2 to cover the first team's entry. Their job would be to fire the concussion grenades and tear gas and then assume preplanned positions around the exterior perimeter of the house. They would then await orders from the first A Team. The plan was, once the initial assault team made entry, they would clear the building room by room. Once a room was cleared, individual members of A Team 2 would enter and secure each room so that members of the first A Team could continue their search and rescue operation. Speed was essential to a successful operation. All were aware that Sanders had told negotiators that he was standing next to Hester holding a handgun and that if anyone attempted to rescue him he would blow his head off. A little after 3:00 a.m., a "Signal Blue" was given out over the radio. This was the code that authorized the mission to begin. A thunder of noise exploded as members of the second assault team fired many rounds of both concussion grenades and tear gas into virtually all windows and doorways. Some were also shooting shotguns loaded with ferret rounds inside the windows to add to the confusion. Simultaneously, the members of A Team 1 entered the house from the rear doorway, the same doorway that Officer Aiken had entered repeatedly in his attempts to rescue Officers Schwill and Hester. Officers Hubbard and Ray were responsible for using the battering ram to knock down the rear door. Their objective was to get the door down and then fall behind the fourth man to enter, who was Officer McNair, the overall team leader. Officer Watson was the first in the door, followed by Officers Rutherford, Watson and Summers, and then McNair. Conditions inside the house were bad. The power had been turned off the night before so it had gotten very cold inside. It was also very dark as no lights could be used. In addition to these problems, the first assault team would be blinded by the tear gas and the smoke. They had taped flashlights to the ends of their weapons, which was a tactic that had been learned from some of the veterans who had served in Vietnam. Rails, common today for the mounting of flashlights and other accessories to assault weapons, were not available at the time, so officers had to devise their own means to utilize whatever they could come up with to increase officer safety.

As they entered, they immediately began taking fire from various locations throughout the house. They were wearing gas masks, which restricted their already-hampered vision. Clouds of gas and smoke drifted everywhere. The first officer inside witnessed movement near the floor in a doorway and saw a suspect holding a weapon pointed in his direction. He fired a number of times with his M16, striking the subject, which halted all movement from this threat. The entry team was told to expect suspects to be crawling on the floor to escape the tear gas. He then cautiously entered the room, followed closely by his backup, Officer Rutherford, and saw another subject which he fired upon. After that threat was eliminated, he saw another two male blacks already down near the two that he had shot. These were also eliminated. Continuing the sweep throughout the house, they saw Officer Hester near the front door. He was laying face down and his wrists were handcuffed behind his back. Two officers, still wearing their protective gas masks, grabbed Officer Hester and ran through the front door. They gently placed him on the front lawn, called for medics, and hurried back inside in order to continue clearing the property. Many officers around the perimeter witnessed this action and were moved by it. Most of them were unable to identify the body as they raced past it on their way inside. One said later that he could not even tell whether the body on the lawn was white or black because there was so much blood about the head. Standing over the body, one officer commented later that the only way he could tell the race was when he noticed his handcuffed wrists, which showed white skin above the partially rolled-up sleeves. It was impossible to tell by simply looking at his head. Blood and heavy bruising had mostly obscured his facial features.

Officer McNair crossed into the hallway behind the first two officers and took fire from in front of him. He was carrying a shotgun and spun and fired in the direction of the fire. Meanwhile, Officer Rutherford had heard the sounds of gunfire from the hallway and raced back into it to assist Officer McNair. He fired at the threat in order to neutralize any further firing.

Officer Hildre Ray was the fifth man inside Shannon Street. After using the battering ram to knock down the rear door, Officer Ray, followed closely by Hubbard, joined the team already inside to offer them cover as they cautiously swept through the house. After securing the first room they entered, the den with the bar, they then entered the hallway leading to the rest of the house. Down the hallway, he entered the first bedroom and saw a closet that could have been hiding one or more of the suspects. They cleared this room without incident, and from it, they could peer into the next bedroom. Ray did this and saw a male subject, armed with a .38-caliber pistol pointing at the doorway. He paused a moment and then jumped into the doorway and fired a round from the shotgun he was carrying. He then saw the man go down. He saw more people inside this room, but they were all down and not moving. He watched these subjects for a couple of minutes, and after deciding that they were not a threat, he proceeded down the hallway to provide backup cover for the other officers. Ray followed the officers into the living room area and saw Officer Hester on the floor. He watched as two officers lifted Hester up and carried him through the front door. There was no doubt in his mind about the condition of Officer Hester. They were too late. Hester was dead. While this was going on, Officer Ray began to feel pain in his right hand. Adrenaline had prevented him from noticing that anything was wrong before this. Another officer, most likely McNair, also noticed Ray's injury and ordered him out of the house. He was escorted to the front door, the same door that Hester had been carried out, and was taken to the hospital via ambulance for treatment. Officer Ray had suffered the painful injury while using the battering ram on the back door. He had caught his hand between the ram and the doorway while making the initial entry. He had a number of broken fingers and serious cuts and abrasions. In his report, Officer Ray stated that he heard many rounds being fired at the entry team. He identified these rounds as coming from a handgun of some sort, and since none of the entry team members were carrying side arms as their primary weapons, they knew these were hostile rounds. While all team members carried side arms, all carried either M16 rifles or shotguns. At no time did any of the officers discharge their department-issued handguns.

Officer Don Rutherford had been a member of the Memphis Police Department for twelve years at the time the Shannon Street assault took place. He had spent the last seven years as a member of the TACT team. Rutherford was the second officer to enter the house. He, like the rest of his team, began taking fire from inside the house from the hallway. Rutherford felt a crushing blow hit him in the back, and he went down forcefully. He staggered and laid prone on the floor for a short time trying to figure out what had happened to him. His mind was racing. He knew he had been hit, but had no idea to what extent he was injured. He never lost consciousness and didn't feel any real pain. He tested all his limbs one by one, and they all worked. He also felt for blood and could not find any. He later stated that he was either shot in the back or that perhaps one of the tear gas canisters or concussion grenades had struck him as he made his way through the den. The blow knocked him off his feet, but fortunately for him, he was wearing two bulletproof vests, which most likely saved his life.

After he had regained his bearings, he got back on his feet. Crossing in front of the hallway, Rutherford saw muzzle flashes and heard rounds being fired in his direction. The darkness was so intense that he could clearly see the flashes, but not who was firing at them. He aimed his M16 with the flashlight at the muzzle flashes and could make out only a hand that was holding a weapon through the smoke and haze. He fired off a few rounds and ducked away, finding cover behind some debris. He cautiously entered the main hallway and came to a doorway leading into a bedroom where he felt that the subject he had just fired upon had fled. He was right. He sensed movement inside the room and ordered his men to halt. He glanced into the room and again saw movement and fired at it. Later, it was determined that the movement he witnessed was nothing more than shadows. All the windows in the home had been shattered, and there was a strong breeze that was making the window coverings move. He then entered the living room and saw Officer Hester lying on the floor near the doorway. He sprinted to his side and saw that he was obviously dead. He screamed to the officers outside that they had found Hester and were bringing him outside. He, along with another officer, then carried Hester outside and placed him just off the porch. The doctor who had been called to the scene ran to Hester's aid, and it did not take him long to pronounce him dead. Rutherford ordered the doctor to seek cover and reentered the house through the front door. There was nothing further that could be done for Officer Hester, but there still were subjects inside the home that they had to deal with. All had refused to surrender after having been given repeated opportunities to do so. If they had so brutally murdered a police officer, then not one member of the assault teams believed that there would be a peaceful climax forthcoming. Under normal circumstances, when entering a building during an assault, the entry team methodically searches and clears each area one at a time. That was the original plan at Shannon Street, but initially, this was not done because of two reasons:

1. They were intent upon rescuing Officer Hester who they believed could still be alive.
2. Since Hester and Schwill had been ambushed earlier and thirty hours of negotiations had produced nothing in the way of compromise from the hostage takers, the entry team felt strongly that another ambush was going to happen. Also, when they heard the construction taking place inside earlier,

most thought that barricades were being built in order to thwart any rescue attempt.

Subsequently, they were intent upon isolating the threats while at the same time securing the fallen officer. A more thorough search would be done as soon as the premises were more secure, after the initial sweep. During the second sweep, Officer Rutherford proceeded back down the hallway. Peering into a room at the end, he saw a subject scooting across the floor attempting to get to a weapon. Rutherford fired on this subject, killing him. Two officers in front of Rutherford saw another man behind a bed and traded fire with him. Neither officer was hit in the exchange but the subject was killed.

All the rooms in the house had been secured, but the officers were very concerned about someone possibly hiding in the attic. They began to search for an entryway into the attic but could not find it. Officer Rutherford then pulled down some ceiling tiles in the den and climbed up on the bar. He poked his head into the attic and, with the flashlight still taped to his rifle, searched the attic. He found nothing. All the subjects had been hiding on the main floor of the ranch-style home. After completing the search, room by room, the A Team called for the backup team to enter. They did so, and each member of the backup team was assigned a room to guard. Rutherford and the rest of the first team then left the building and proceeded to the command post, which had been relocated to a house a couple of doors down from 2239 Shannon Street. Before retiring to the command post, Rutherford assisted in carrying the slain officer, Bobby Hester, to the waiting ambulance. They placed him on a stretcher and gently carried him away. After spending some time at the command post, he realized that his M16 was missing. He had lain it down on the grass in order to get Hester in the ambulance. He quickly retrieved his rifle. When asked later how many rounds he had fired, Rutherford stated forty to forty-five. The M16 had a magazine that held thirty rounds, and he did reload once during the assault so this number is plausible.

Officer C. R. Summers was also a thirteen-year veteran of the Memphis Police Department. He had served the last seven years as a member of the TACT team. When he arrived on the scene, he was teamed up with Officer Cockrell who had taken up a position in the house next door to 2239. They were both stationed near a window directly across from a bedroom at 2239 where they could clearly hear Officer Hester. They listened for hours as Bobby Hester cried out in agony from the vicious beating that he was taking. He was crying and begging for mercy while at least two, and perhaps more, individuals continued to beat and torture him unmercifully. He was pleading with them not to kill him. He once screamed, "Oh, God, please no, oh God." Summers constantly relayed updates of this beating to the command staff over his radio, which had a Channel 10. The radios Schwill and Hester carried did not receive Channel 10, so there was no way that the subjects inside could hear what Summers was relaying. He remained at this location up until an hour or so before the assault order was given. He, like many others present, could not understand why nothing was being done to save Hester. Summers was so close he thought he could have gotten into the room where Hester was being held with only a few short strides. He was anxious to go.

Summers was a last-minute replacement on the team. He was to be the third man to enter the house, right behind Officer Rutherford. Once he and the rest of his team entered the house, they began taking fire instantly. While seeking cover from the incoming rounds, a concussion grenade went off close to where he was crouched. It temporarily blinded him, which is what its intended purpose was, and the bright flash of light in the deeply darkened room totally ruined his night vision. Besides being blinded, the grenade stunned him. No grenades or tear gas were supposed to be fired into the house once the initial team made its entry. Obviously, someone screwed up, but in a maneuver like this one, which required pinpoint accuracy and timing, mistakes were bound to occur. Most likely, it was one of these rounds that struck Officer Rutherford in the back knocking him flat. As Summers was regaining his night vision, he began systematically sweeping the house; he came across the body of Officer Hester in the distance lying on the floor near the front door. He, along with his partner, Rutherford, yelled to the officers outside around the perimeter that they were coming out with Hester.

After placing Hester on the ground outside, he and Rutherford reentered the house to renew the search. He came to a doorway and peered inside. He could not see much of anything as, along with the tear gas, a couple of fires had begun to burn inside. In the living room, the sofa had begun to smolder from one of the tear gas grenades that had been launched into the area. It was a small fire, but the smoke it was creating was thick and intense. He saw the fire, but there were more pressing matters to be dealt with.

When Summers approached the entranceway to the bedroom, he could make out a circular-shaped bed in the haze. He first checked out the closet and then he approached the bed, and he could see something in the rear, behind the bed, but he could not easily get to it. He called for assistance to help move it out of the way. It would be much safer to simply move the bed out of the way than to stick a flashlight underneath it and look. He then jumped up onto the bed and saw a male black suspect lying on the floor behind the bed. The subject had a pistol in his hand and opened fire on Officer Summers. Summers returned fire, and the subject dropped the pistol and slumped to the floor, dead. Not knowing if he was dead or alive, in fact if he even hit him, Summers retrieved the pistol and threw it up on the bed out of the reach of the gunman. He then proceeded to search the room one last time and then called for one of the backup team officers to secure the bedroom, which turned out to be the master bedroom. It is possible that this subject had been wounded earlier. There is no way to determine if he had been injured or not when he confronted Officer Summers.

When Summers originally arrived on the scene, he was advised that the two officers had been responding to a disturbance call and had been taken hostage. Later on, he was told that the entire scenario involving Hester and Schwill had been a devious setup on the part of the people inside. Who exactly gave him this information has never been determined. He was also told that Officer Tommy Turner had received lacerations to his scalp and had been admitted to the hospital. He was also informed that one officer had been shot twice, once with a small caliber handgun and then a second time at point-blank range to the head with the officer's own weapon. There was a lot of speculation on the part of many at the scene. Rumors were spreading like wildfire. No one could be certain what exactly was fact or fiction. Could this entire scenario have been an intentional setup on the part of Lindberg Sanders? That possibility was seriously considered and discarded pretty quickly. No one ever really believed that Sanders planned the entire confrontation. He had been preaching of the coming of the end of the world for days. He had told his wife about it, and many of his followers had told their loved ones that they thought they might not ever be returning home. Sanders believed in the forthcoming apocalypse, but I doubt that even he knew in what form it would be coming. Certainly, for him and his followers, he was correct.

Patrolman Robert Watson was the final member of the original assault entry team. He was the first officer since Russ Aiken almost twenty-four hours earlier to make entry into the house. In fact, Russ Aiken was consulted by the team before they made entry. Since he had been the only one to actually enter the house from the rear, on a number of different occasions, he was able to provide the team with invaluable intelligence prior to their assault. Aiken told them about the bar they would confront once they entered the rear door. Aiken, in fact, had leaped over this very same bar as he withdrew in order to reload his weapon. He had become intimately familiar with it in a very short period of time. His contribution was, once again, critical to the success of the rescue attempt. Watson's primary initial objective was to secure the bar area and to make certain no one was hiding behind it. Ambush was at the top of the list in terms of the danger they faced. As soon as he, along with the rest of the team, made entry, they were fired upon from within the confines of the house. Once again, the team had to endure the apparent tardiness of the shooters outside. A number of concussion grenades and tear gas canisters were still being fired into the house with the team already inside. This firing was supposed to cease once entry made been made. But with everything that had occurred over the course of the last thirty hours, it is easy to see why it happened. Everyone wanted to do their part. Everyone wanted to finally rescue Officer Hester. The entire entry team all had to take cover to avoid not only the rounds being fired at them from inside the house, but also the grenades and tear gas being lobbed by the officers on the outside. The timing simply broke down. Finally, the room was cleared and the sweep began. Watson entered another room that had a refrigerator inside, obviously the kitchen. He noticed a pair of shoes behind the open refrigerator door and opened fire at the door. It later turned out that Officer Watson had indeed shot the refrigerator door. But that is all that there was, a simple pair of shoes someone had placed at the base of the refrigerator. He then exited that room and proceeded to another room where he noticed a male black lying on the floor with a gun either in his hand or within easy reaching distance and fired a round at this subject. Another officer was entering the same room from a different doorway and saw the same subject on the floor with the gun. He fired at the same time Officer Watson let loose with his M16. The suspect was down and the threat eliminated. He had probably been shot additionally by other members during the initial assault, but the true determination is impossible to make.

Among all the team members was the hope that Officer Hester was still alive when they made entry. They went out of their way to hold fire unless they were fired upon themselves. They had no desire to possibly mistakenly shoot the officer who had suffered so horribly throughout this entire ordeal. This was the primary reason, but most certainly not the only reason, that they had methodically taped flashlights to barrels of their weapons. Offers to surrender had been shouted as they systematically cleared each room, but no response was ever heard from anyone.

Officer Watson then entered another bedroom where he noticed a pistol lying on top of a bed. Upon investigation, he saw a male black lying behind the bed and that this subject had been shot in the head and that he was obviously dead. Watson was in full tactical gear including his vest, armored helmet, gas mask, and other utility gear. Since the property had not been completely secured, he left the handgun lying on the bed and exited the room. He did not want to contaminate any crime scene by touching the weapon. The threat had been eliminated, so it made sense to leave it alone and continue the sweep. He then came across the body of Patrolman Hester near the front door. After the removal of Hester's body from the scene, Watson had initially determined that he was dead because he was not moving and his body was cold to the touch, even with his heavy gloves on. Watson reentered the house to complete the sweep of the premises.

The assault had been completed. Regrettably, Hester had not been found alive. The team members had been anticipating this scenario, but when confronted with the evidence, they were all devastated. When exactly Hester died is not certain, but what is certain is that the officer had been dead for some time prior to the rescue attempt. All the officers on the scene were crushed. Most had been on the scene, off and on, since the beginning, some thirty-plus hours earlier. They had all heard the screaming coming from inside the house, and they were hopeful that once the order was finally given to attempt the rescue, that the eventual outcome would be a good one. Obviously, this was not to be the case. Hester was dead, and all seven remaining hostage takers inside the house had been killed. A tremendous feeling permeated throughout all the officers, from the lowliest patrolman to the director himself that they had failed. The morale of the cops could not have been lower. Many officers were seen crying and hugging each other. What else could they have done? Police Union President Ray Maples was interviewed on the scene and heavily criticized the police brass. He had been there the entire time, and he felt that the safety and security of all the rank and file was his responsibility. He carries this burden with him to this day. Interviewing Ray at the preaching school he was attending in suburban Germantown, Tennessee, I could not help but notice the pain in his eyes when he spoke of Shannon Street twenty-five years after the fact. Maples is now in poor health, and no doubt, the guilt he carries with him over Hester's death only helps to worsen his condition. Maples has nothing to feel guilty about. He had no command authority on the scene. He was simply another patrolman who was forced to witness the most tragic incident in the history of the Memphis Police Department. Every man there those two fateful days in January shoulders a burden that no one should ever have to deal with. All found a way to handle it, and some better than others. Certainly all were affected. It took many years for the morale of the department to improve. Now Shannon Street is a distant memory to most. The twenty-fifth anniversary of the incident was on January 13, 2008, and the local television stations all did reports on it. There were interviews with attorneys and officers who were there. Perhaps the most emotional was the interview given by Ray Maples, now with the life-threatening health issues that he has to deal with. Maples, long since retired, sat in his living room and criticized the command staff for not allowing the officers on the scene to attempt a rescue of Officer Hester sooner. You could see in his pain-racked eyes, as they teared up, the torment he had been enduring for all these years. Counter this with interviews given by certain members of the ambulance-chasing, race-baiting members of the legal profession who only see dollar signs to be gained by this tragedy. A sad testimony, indeed, on the city wracked with racial tension even after all these years that some members of the community cannot let go of. They see an opportunity to chase a dollar. Had they been there that terrible night and seen the pain and agony, I doubt they would be reacting the same way.

CHAPTER 28

Aftermath

One wonders what must have been going through the mind of Officer Hester that night. He was an experienced officer with many years on the department. He had been involved in countless circumstances far more dangerous than the initial call to investigate a purse snatching. No doubt he anticipated another typical call with little danger involved. As he approached the doorway with his partner, the cold winter night was made worse by a brisk wind coming in from the north. When they stepped onto the porch and knocked on the door, they had no reason to believe that this call was going to be any different than any other. They were invited into the small living room and were surprised to find all those men sitting around. They could sense hostility in the air, and their training immediately kicked in. Gain the upper hand. Dominate the environment; take command of the situation. Be strong and forceful. Show you're tough, and that you are to be obeyed. This tactic, which usually worked flawlessly in the past, failed them this night. Following proper police procedure (and common sense), the officers did the right thing; they tried to get the man they wanted to talk with, out of the house and away from all those people. They succeeded in doing so, and it was actually on the front lawn where Officer Schwill was assaulted first. Hester was near the front door when he was overwhelmed. Neither one of them could have seen it coming. Hester, who had to have felt the tension and hostility while in the house with all those men, most likely breathed a sigh of relief when he saw that things were going to be taken outside. No doubt Schwill was also relieved to see things heading outdoors. The shock of being struck had to have been overwhelming. He knew his partner was also under attack on the front lawn, and it was impossible for either one to come to the aid of the other. At some point, the shock of being physically attacked was replaced by confusion, fear, anger, and helplessness, not necessarily in that order. Schwill had been successful in getting two radio calls out for help. They knew other cops were racing to their location. Would they arrive in time? Neither had no way of knowing, but just knowing that help would be there momentarily had to have given them so comfort. If they could only hold out long enough for help to arrive. They walked up to the front door and, within a couple of minutes, were in the fight of their lives. No one attacked cops like this. What was happening? Why were they the ones being assaulted? It was nothing more than a bogus call about a purse snatching. Questions like these must have been running, albeit briefly, through the minds of the officers. Now they were locked in a life or death struggle against overwhelming numbers.

Help finally did arrive and within minutes. By this time, Hester had been dragged into a side room and was screaming for his partner to "come get me." His partner was in no condition to help anyone. He was forcibly dragged back into the house right behind Hester where he was systematically being beaten and kicked. He struggled to get his gun or to at least prevent his attackers from getting it, but there were simply too many of them. He was overpowered, and during the struggle, his gun went off with the bullet entering the palm of his hand and exiting out the top. The pain had to have been excruciating, but with all the adrenaline pumping through his body, he probably felt little. He was on his hands and knees, still struggling, because he knew he had to get out of there. Staying inside the house was a death sentence, and Schwill knew this. As he tried to push himself up off his knees, one of the men standing over him fired. The bullet struck Schwill in the head, entering just behind his ear and exiting out the lower jaw. He went down immediately. A horrendous-looking wound that bled terribly. He fell back to the ground and pretended to play dead. He was still being kicked, even while pretending to be dead, when gunfire erupted from the back of the house. Whoever was kicking him ran to the sound of the gunshots, and the rest of his attackers scattered. Out of the corner of his eye, he glanced around the room and could only see one attacker, who was peering outside, not paying any attention to him. This man could not see Schwill from where he was, and Schwill made the decision that ultimately saved his life. He had been harnessing his energy waiting for this moment, and he was prepared. His mind was racing to formulate a plan that would get him out of danger. Playing dead had been working for the moment, but he knew he had to get out of there. With the lone attacker's attention still toward the outside, Schwill made a leap toward the front door and pushed his way out of the house. He landed in the arms of other officers who were surprised when the door flew open. They got Schwill under cover and rushed him to the hospital.

Now there was one left to save. Officer Bobby Hester remained inside the house. Gunfire was erupting from both inside and outside the house. He was being systematically beaten until the gunfire erupted. When everyone scattered, Hester did not have the same opportunity that Schwill did to escape. He had been handcuffed with his hands behind his back with his own handcuffs. Whether this was done before or after the shooting began is uncertain. He may have been rendered temporarily unconscious by the initial beating he took. Either way, the odds were stacked against Officer Hester. While Schwill was being beaten in the front room of the property, only a few short steps from the front door, Hester had been taken into a bedroom off to the side. He would have to run out the bedroom door, through the living room, and out the front door in order to escape. All this while being handicapped by the handcuffs tightly securing his arms behind his back. There was a window in the room that he could have possibly leaped through, but it was not very large, and to jump through it, while injured and handcuffed with your hands behind your back, would have made it next to impossible. His best shot at escape in those first few moments of utter confusion was the front door, the same door that Schwill ran out of. He never got the chance.

What was going through the mind of Officer Hester at that point in time? We will never know for certain as he took all that with him to his grave. Possibly he was wondering when the help that he knew to be outside at this time due to all the gunfire was going to burst in the door and rescue him. He knew he was injured. He no doubt thought about Officer Schwill as he had no way to know for certain if he had made it out or what kind of condition he was in. He must have been praying heavily by this time. Knowing that his rescuers were only a few short feet away had to have given him hope. He had been taught in the academy that your partners and the department were always going to be there for you. You never left one of your own behind. He could hear sounds that much we know for certain. He was being systematically beaten, and he had to have been confused by everything. Why were these men torturing him? Why didn't the department and his brother officers overwhelm the house and rescue him? Why was this happening to him? As the hours passed, he could see the utter determination in his captors. He could hear his tormentors talking with the police outside. He had been yelling for the officers to rescue him. He could see and feel the cold fury all around him. He had to have known that as the hours dragged on; unless a rescue was imminent, he was in serious trouble. Lindberg Sanders was psychologically unbalanced before this all began. Now on top of that, he was seriously injured having been shot in the forearm during Officer Russ Aiken's heroic initial charge into the house. As the beatings continued, Sanders continued acting more and more irrational. Hester knew that help was there. He didn't know why it was taking so long. He could hear Sanders's rants. He overheard Sanders demand to speak to a disc jockey live on the air so that he could "blow this motherfucker's head off." He must have felt abandoned by the department he had served so faithfully for all those years. He probably died wondering why.

RAMIFICATIONS

After the assault ended and Officer Hester's body was finally taken from the residence, the Memphis Police Department sent in a team to chronicle, photograph, and videotape everything in the house. Meticulous notes and diagrams were drawn outlining the horrific events that had taken place. When the dust finally settled, six bodies were found in one room. They were head to toe together almost in a neat row. The men were found with the second lying at the feet of the first, the next one lying at the head, and so forth. The seventh body was discovered in a bedroom next to a round bed with a white bedspread. A gun was discovered on the bed above where the body lay. When this was all made public, during an in-depth press conference held by the chief, John Holt, there was outrage from some people in and out of the black community. The cry of racism was heard over and over again. A local political activist and head of the local chapter of the NAACP, Maxine Waters, demanded a full-scale federal investigation. A local Memphis activist, Lance Watson, also known as known as Sweet Willie Wine on the street and Minster Abdul, organized a march held a few days later at the house on Shannon. In support of what he began calling the Shannon Seven, no doubt capitalizing on the historic Chicago Seven during the 1960s. A few dozen people showed up, along with local and network news organizations, and after film was taken and the cameras left, the demonstration broke up peacefully. The police director, John Holt, held an in-depth press conference and gave a moment-by-moment account of the thirty hours from the time of the first call to the eventual end. He gave a prepared statement to the press. His statement read as follows:

Ladies and gentlemen, I'm going to read a prepared statement at this point. In this statement I think I've included as much information as I can at this point in time. Of course, the investigation is still very active, officers are still on the scene, so to go beyond what I have here, I will not be able to do so.

On Tuesday, January 11, 1983, at approximately 9 p.m., Officers R.O. Schwill and R.S. Hester received a call to 2239 Shannon. The call was from a male who advised the operator that he hadn't done anything, but he wanted to talk to the Police. It is believed that this call was placed in order to lure the Officers into this situation.

After Officers Schwill and Hester made the scene, the entered the house at 2239 Shannon and were immediately jumped by numerous persons. The Officers were able to call for help and other cars were dispatched to the scene. During the initial encounter, Officer Schwill was shot in the face and hand by one of the subjects in the house. Officer Tommy Turner, who responded to a call for help, was struck in the head and disabled and had to be taken to the hospital. Several shots were fired at Officer W.R. Aiken, who was able to return fire and escape. Based on statements by Officer Aiken, we believe that at least one of the subjects was hit at this time.

The area was sealed off and the TACT Squad and the hostage negotiating team responded to the scene and efforts began to negotiate the release of the officer.

During the early morning hours of Wednesday, January 12, negotiators heard what sounded to be a subject using a Police radio taken from the Officer.

Attempts were made to negotiate over the radio, in addition to using the bullhorn and attempting to establish telephone contact.

During this time from approximately midnight till 4:00 A.M. (Wednesday) there were indications from the officer inside that the officer was being brutalized.

However, the decision was made at this time not to attempt to assault the house since it was believed that a pistol was being held to the Officers head and entry could not be gained without meaning certain death to the officer.

Repeated attempts were made to negotiate, but the occupant refused to respond. Observation posts were placed in adjoining houses and voices were heard. One voice in particular, believed to be that of Lindberg Sanders, was shouting obscenities and threats against the officer's life.

Negotiation effort continued, but no demands were received and officers were unable to determine what the subjects wanted.

At approximately 7:00 a.m. on Wednesday morning, negotiators heard the Officer call out "Give them whatever they want." No further word was heard from the officer during the daylight hours Wednesday.

At approximately 11:00 p.m. Wednesday evening, the Memphis Police Department placed two microphones (inside the house) which allowed the MPD to listen to conversations inside the house. The bullhorn was also used to inquire as to the health of the police officer hostage and other occupants since it was believed one or more may have been struck during the initial exchange of gunfire.

A voice, the same one head most frequently, that his daddy was dead, his brother was dead, and the devil was dead, apparently referring to the police officer as "The Devil."

Shortly after, the same voice commented about being cold and bleeding from the arm. Monitors were able to pick up sounds of nausea inside the dwelling and it is believed these sounds were made by one of the occupants.

Shortly thereafter, another effort was made to contact the occupants but the only sound received were moans.

In view of the information available and the possibility that some deaths had already occurred, plus the possibility that the voice that was heard belonged to a person that was injured, the decision was made to force entry into the home.

Also considered was the refusal of the occupants to communicate or negotiate in any manner.

At approximately 3:00 a.m. this date, forcible entry was undertaken by the TACT Squad, and several tear gas grenades were injected into the house. Members of the TACT Squad storming the front door were fired on as they entered the living room of the house. Gunfire was returned by the TACT Squad.

The battered body of the police officer was found just inside the front door. His hands were cuffed behind his back. There were indications that he had been dead for a number of hours.

As the TACT squad members proceeded through the house, they were again met by gunfire as they reached the second room. The gunfire was returned.

There were seven male blacks inside the house, all of whom were fatally shot. Identification of these persons are being withheld pending notification of next of kin.

The medical examiner has determined that all seven of these persons were killed during the assault.

During this ordeal, the Memphis Police Department has attempted to utilize the accepted principles of negotiations which dictate that negotiations or attempts to negotiate, continue as long as there is a reasonable indication that the hostage is alive.

When the indications were that the officers, and possibly others, were injured or dead, the decision was made to force entry into the house. Ladies and gentlemen, that is all I will be able to say at this time. As additional information becomes available, we will make it available to you.

After he released this statement, he promised to hold an in-depth news conference shortly.

The story was big news locally and nationally for a few days. The national media eventually abandoned the story. Local media also moved on to other stories. It seemed, at least for a while, that the city and its citizens wanted nothing more than to put the whole ugly incident behind them. But the story would not die. Ms. Waters and others continued to call for a federal investigation utilizing investigators from outside the city of Memphis. She released a statement that read as follows:

I called for the investigation so that an impartial investigation other than that the Police Department could be conducted. It is the nature of the police department to use guns and violence and I think that the Justice Department should begin an immediate investigation.

She wanted people from Washington, DC, to head up the investigation. Interestingly enough, the head of the national chapter of the NAACP was quoted on network television as saying that it appeared that the police acted responsibly. The local chapter took issue with this and continued to press for a national investigation. Naturally, the Memphis Police Department launched their own investigation. It was promised by the director that it would be in-depth and completely impartial. The eyes of the world were upon the city of Memphis and its administration. They were committed to reveal the truth, but only after every stone had been uncovered. They would not be pressured into releasing an incomplete report.

Memphis City Councilman Bob James released a statement in full support of the police department and their actions in dealing with the crisis on Shannon Street. He stated, "How much consideration should you give seven animals who were in there torturing a policeman?" Ms. Smith retaliated by stating, "That statement made by James is symbolic of what most of the feelings, attitudes, and actions of the police department of Memphis. It shows a complete lack of value that is placed on the black life in the community."

Director Holt was continuously updating the press and public. The director held an in-depth press conference and answered all questions put forth by the media. A transcript of that press conference is as follows:

Holt began the briefing by stating:

We feel our officers are entitled to an in depth investigation of what occurred. And I hope I've been able to give that to you today. I don't know what else I could tell you. I've tried to be as complete and detailed as possible. I will entertain questions if they are pertinent or on something I can answer.

Q. One of them were the officer's revolver?

A. Both Were.

Q. So the people weren't armed when the police got there the first time?

A. No, we don't know that. Remember there were seven individuals that left. The first officers on the scene, thought, well they were fired on. We know that. We know they were fired on a number of times. So there is a strong possibility . . .

Q. So you thing somebody—one of the ones who left—took some weapons with them, or at least a weapon?

A. It is very possible that some weapons left. During the course of the negotiation period we were never able to determine, we were receiving contradictory information—well not really contradictory. We had a number of people, or some people telling us, Yes there are other weapons in the house; these people are hunters so they have shotguns; they have rifles, but also during this period of time we had other people who had been in the house say "Well, I've never seen them there." We do think there was a very strong possibility that other weapons did leave the house.

Q. In concluding that your officers acted correctly on the initial contact, and also on the sweep through the residence by members of the TACT squad, what more could have been done; what will you do differently in the future on a situation like this?

A. I have relived these hours many times. I don't know of a thing we could have done differently. I don't know of a thing the officers that responded could have done differently. They went to this address in response to a call from a citizen. They had no idea that there was any agitation, any resentment against them. They were sent there by the dispatcher to investigate a complaint and based on their statement, which is corroborated by the statement of people in the house, by 14 of them and from that point on, the matter was out of our hands.

Q. Did your officers ask people in the house to surrender or did they ask them to throw down their weapons upon entering?

A. No, On the assault?

Q. Yes Sir.

A. No sir. We had spent 30 hours trying to get the people to talk to us, surrender, cooperate—all of which had been futile. And at that particular point in time, and I've discussed the thought process that went into the decision to assault. I think we were, for the benefit of everyone concerned, our people going in the house, plus the officer that was already in there. It was absolutely essential that the maneuver was accomplished as rapidly as possible.

Q. Do you still believe your presentation that all seven people in the house were participant?

A. There's no question in my mind. We know that at the very outset, half the group left.

Q. Officer Schwill was shot with his own revolver, is that right?

A. That's correct.

Q. So the only guns that you know that were actually in the house that you have positive information about were the two police revolvers?

A. That's Correct.

Q. Now you say that seven people left and you also said that perhaps some guns left the house. Well, leaving the scene of a crime and taking with, I assume, is a criminal act. Is anyone going to be charged with anything? Has anyone been charged with anything?

A. That's still under investigation.

Q. During the last few hours we heard a report that the police were up, that this whole thing was a setup that the officers were there responding to a call. From what you've told us does it appear to you that they were actually set up? Or did this whole thing perhaps evolve from a misunderstanding on the part of Sanders, who became outraged when the officers arrived?

A. Any evidence would indicate that there was a plan, a group plan. I think from listening to the tapes we played here—particularly the one made from the dispatcher—I think it is very evident that the voice in the background that that person was extremely agitated. He was cursing, wanted the officers out there right then, which indicates to us that at least in his mind—if not in the minds of the other people—they were going to punish the officer for what they perceived to be an insult.

Q. Did the seven who left the house take Officer Hester's weapon?

A. We heard that report. We have not been able to find any indication, as a matter of fact, Sanders . . .

Q. Is it reasonable to assume that you too have learned late, that the guns exchanged hands during the chaos?

A. I think it is reasonable to assume. We listened as the people . . . could be taken, would certainly permit . . . The one is injured . . . the one who dropped . . .

Q. Just to clarify, how many victims do you believe had guns in their hands when they were shot by the police?
A. We know that this one had a gun in his hand. We know this one had a gun in his hand, and this one. Is that right? (Holt is pointing to photographs)

Q. Three of the seven had guns?
A.—

Q. What discussion did you have to bring the capture about?

A. Considerable discussion. Just prior to the assault, I went over and met with the TACT commanders—with the people in the TAC unit. And it was discussed in detail as to how they would be brought out, where they would be taken for immediate search and security, and how they were to be transported from here. We spent 15 minutes, I guess, discussing, and this was just prior to the assault.

Q. The man who is in custody, what is he accused of doing? I know what the charges are, but . . . what about suspects?

A. I think I answered that, 24 rounds, 24 rounds is what they started with.

Q. And all those came from police officers?

A. I think they started off with 24 rounds of police ammunition, is that correct? Twenty four rounds they started with. They started with 24 rounds of police ammunition, and that's the only hulls we discovered.

Q. How many were expended, all 24"

A. We recovered 12 expended hulls.

Q. Director, at the beginning of the news conference you said you believed there were 25 members of this cult here in Memphis. What is happening with the remaining 18 members? And have you talked to all these people?

A. No, we haven't talked with all of them. And beyond their involvement in a criminal incident we are restricted by Federal consent decree from accumulating any intelligence information on an organization of that sort. It's something I would like to ask our city attorney to review to see if it's possible to modify in any way. But the prohibition on the department at this point is absolutely against accumulating any domestic intelligence information.

Q. Are they considered a threat?

A. Regardless of their beliefs until they are thought to be involved in actual criminal activity, we are forbidden from accumulating or investigating this type of organization.

Q. Let's get this verified one last time. There were 12 rounds shot by the victims, fired by the victims in this case. How many were fired by police officers?

A. About 80 rounds.

Q. How many weapons? How many officers participated in the assault and what weapons did they use?

A. I gave you the names of the officers, and that's all of them. There were six officers four M-16's and two shotguns.

Q. Director, has the police department reinstituted the stop and search on the street practice as a precaution?

A. I beg your pardon?

Q. The stop and search practice. Has it been reinstituted by the police department as a result of this?

A. No, we haven't modified our normal policies or procedures. They're in effect pretty well prescribed by law.

Q. There's no new precautions instituted by the police department?

A. No.

Q. Director, what about the death threats that have been coming in supposedly since shortly after 3 O'clock Thursday morning. Do you think that's part of the other people in this cult or do you think that's completely separate?

A. It would be speculation. I'm not sure I understood. You're talking about other threats?

Q. Yes, I understand that a number of death threat have been coming in to the police department.

A. It would be speculation. I personally wouldn't think there was any connection. Do we have anything that's really relevant to the matter at hand and not speculation?

Q. Director, they were several local black community leaders who offered to assist to try to negotiate with these people. However, as far as I know they were not used. Was that considered?

A. Oh, yes I'm glad you brought that up. We had a number of people—the neighbors, relatives, leaders from the black community—offering assistance. And we would have utilized an or all those if we had been able to establish an sort of contact The tapes you heard were just the . . . Well, you understand they weren't conversations. They were ravings of an incensed person so had we ever been able to establish, dialogue, yes.

Q. How about the Psychiatrist

A. We talked to a psychiatrist.

Q. He offered his help I understand.

A. We had hundreds of offers of help and we would have gladly . . . as a matter of fact, we did get several people on the phone with him. We got Mac, who is a stepbrother on the phone with him. Unproductive. We got George on the phone, who we had every reason to believe was probably the person that Sanders most respected, on the phone with him. Both very short conversations terminated by Sanders, both totally unproductive.

Q. Director, since this was an incident that never occurred before, is the police department thinking about establishing a policy when another officer is taken hostage?

A. I'm not going to comment on what we might do.

Q. But are you looking into it? I mean, might there be a policy established.

A. I can't say there won't be but I certainly can't say there will be.

Q. Why wasn't police intelligence able to pick up what was going on there? Weren't there any rumblings in the neighborhood that something odd was going on in that house?

A. Prior to all this? As I explained a minute ago, we are forbidden to accumulate or acquire any information on this type of organization or group.

Q. How about individuals?

A. Individuals? We are forbidden.

Q. To the best of your knowledge, had police been called to that address before for anything?

A. I have no idea.

Q. Also, now, you made mention that Mr. Henley would be charged.

A. He has been charged.

Q. Right, okay. Now T.C. Smith got out and there were no charges placed. Why not?

A. Should we respond to that? It's still under investigation.

Q. Was it your decision to make the assault? I may have missed that.

A. I stated that, several times, you know, as director of the police division, certainly it is my responsibility but as I also stated, I had 250 years of police experience backing me up. Of course, as soon as all this occurred, back up units from the police agency began arriving, and I'll just quickly summarize that particular part of it. There were a number of officers, of course, that arrived on the scene. Two of the first were officers Turner and Aiken, who both attempted to enter to assist the officers. Officer Turner started in the front door, and was immediately struck with some object. It's quite possible that he was also struck with the Kale light that had been used to beat officer Hester. At any rate, he received a serious laceration of the head, he was knocked backwards out of the house and had to be removed from the scene. Officer Aiken was able to enter through the rear door in an effort to assist the officers. As he entered he was fired upon and he returned fire. I believe he fired five rounds at that particular point. Officer Aiken believes he saw possibly four weapons at that particular, at that point. He exited the house, reloaded, re-entered. Again, was fired upon, He again emptied his revolver, exited, came back with a shotgun. Attempting to get in to assist the officers. Discharged one or two rounds of the shotgun again, until he was forced to retreat. We had several other officers that were arriving at that time and they were attempting to assist the officers but because of the conditions that existed just were not able to make entry into the house. During this particular time, one of our lieutenants was outside the door, or outside the window. At that point, things were stabilized and they were trying to establish some sort of indications as to who was inside . . . and Lt. Randle heard Lindberg Sanders state that he wanted to be like Light Gas and Water, that he wanted the people of Memphis to hear when he put the officers lights out. So we knew from what had already occurred and from what was said at this particular point that we were in for a very difficult time. We feared at that time the principle interest of the occupants of the house was to do physical harm to the police officers and there didn't appear to be any other reason for the activities that were occurring. We immediately began to attempt to communicate, to try to resolve this, to get the officer out. We knew at that point in time, based on things that had been said by occupants of the house, that our officers had heard plus, and we have some of this on tape, that you'll hear in a minute, that the intent was to execute Officer Hester preferably publicly via the radio. That was the intent in wanting to talk to Mr. C.J. Morgan of WLOK radio, was that he wanted to execute Officer Hester and preferably do it publically via the radio. He wanted to execute officer Hester with the citizens of Memphis listening to the execution. At this point, we made attempts to establish communications with the people inside and determine what we could do to resolve the situation. We were repeatedly told we have nothing that they want, they have what we want. And we were told that any movement on our part would result in the instant death of Officer Hester. (At this point in time, police played a tape of the ravings inside the house. Much of the tape was incomprehensible). Holt continued:

This is a fairly accurate statement of the emotional state of the people we were dealing with at the beginning of the Shannon St. situation. From the information we were getting from the officers close to the house, there was absolutely no question in our mind that any effort would have resulted in instantaneous death to the officer. We also felt that any effort to enter the house at that time would have most probably have resulted in additional injuries to other officers.

There were numerous discussions, meetings, between myself and the rest of the group (meaning the police officers on the stage). I was moving from our command post to another trying to assess the situation . . . ultimately it was my decision, both at this point and later (to go in). I was backed up by 250 years of police experience behind me. During the early stages, we did not feel that the hazard, or certain death of officer Hester, and the probability of serious injury, would permit us to make a rescue attempt at that point.

There wasn't a police officer on the scene or anywhere in the city that wouldn't gladly have taken that risk. But we had a responsibility both to officer Hester, but also to the other men outside. I think that gives you a fair idea of the problem.

In all the training we had in hostage negotiations, the basic policy is to buy time. With time, communications improve. You're able to discover what the hostage takers want. Then negotiations will hopefully resolve the situation. In this case, the rulebook was thrown out. Just the opposite occurred. The communications we were getting on the front end via the radio, and you heard some of the tapes, deteriorated. There was a telephone in the house, but for the most part, the occupants, Mr. Sanders—would leave the phone off the hook. During the hours and hours (of vigilance) we would get through on occasions, but these conversations would be very brief. The statement was made, restated, reiterated, that we did not have a thing that they wanted, that they had what we wanted (Officer Hester). And all they wanted us to do was to come get him.

Q. This term cult has been used rather frequently and loosely. Are you convinced that this is a formal religious organization. I mean, why are you using the term cult, sir?

A. I think I answered that on the front end. Their beliefs would fit the definition of the word cult, but I answered on the front end as far as we know there's no connection or affiliation with any organized group.

Q. Director, now that Sanders has been killed do you believe the cult will continue?

A. I'm not going to get into that sort of discussion at all. If it's relevant to what we're talking about today. I'll try to answer. Otherwise, we've been here too long already.

Q. Director, you have 12 rounds fired altogether from those two service revolvers, but does that include the rounds that were fired during the earlier altercation? Is there any way you can tell what or have those shells been thrown away?

A. No. No. They haven't been thrown away and all that will be part of the continuing investigation.

Q. That's total shells?

A. Total expended.

Q. For both events?

Q. What he I asking is the first confrontation, too. You know when the officers first arrived.

A. Yes

Q. That's total? Twelve shots in the whole deal?

A. Well, no. no. As I pointed out, we recovered 12 expended rounds. We don't know what weapons may have left there between the first confrontation.

Q. Did you find any shells other than 38 caliber shells and shells fired by the tactical officers.

A. No

Q. When you went into the house—the visibility was fairly poor because of the gas.

A. Very poor, certainly.

Q. Well how you explain the accuracy with which these officers were able to shoot all these suspects in the head?

A. I'm glad you asked that question. I should have touched on it during the presentation. The TACT officers, Captain Music, if you will step up to be sure we get it. The TACT officers during their training, of course a considerable part of their training is devoted to night time operations, where in the presence of gas, fog, smoke, whatever, their visibility is going to be very, very restricted. They attach lights to the barrels of the weapons and lights are actually the aiming devices. They are trained, retrained, and trained again to make absolute identification before they fire. It answers some questions that have been brought up about head shots.

An officer in this sort of environment, he's sweeping, his light hits someone, for identification purposes he has to go to the identification area (the head). Once he identifies the subject as a suspect, then he fires. So, in effect, or it's the identification procedure via the use of the light that results in the number of injuries to the head. I'm glad you asked that question, is that a good explanation?

Q. How long did the assault take? You mentioned a momentary pause because of the gas. How long was that pause? How long did the entire thing take?

A. The assault started at 3:06 AM and what's the conclusion time? On the assault? All right, at 3:06 the assault starts. At 3:18 they call for the officer. So during that period they made various sweeps, shots had been fired. So at 3:18 they find the officer, get him out and then I think it's about eight or nine minutes later that they secured except for the attic area.

Q. Chief Holt, street rumor. Was officer Hester's penis cut off?

A. No, absolutely not. No mutilation, absolutely no mutilation. The officer was severely beaten. The injuries he received at the outset had to be very serious. As I stated in the explanation he was struck with a very heavy blow to the head. In all probability he received a fractured skull at that time. But he was beaten, but no bodily mutilation.

Q. The only demand the people made during the whole confrontation was that they wanted the disc jockey over there?

A. But I explained that during the presentation.

Q. I know, why didn't you want him over there?

A. That's exactly what he wanted. He wanted to be on an open mike with Mr. Morgan (the disc jockey) so he could possibly execute the officer.

Q. But the officer was heard to say "give them what they want" which indicates that they had asked for something.

A. They had not. They never made any requests.

Soon after the director held this press conference, Officer Dave Hubbard agreed to an interview with the press. He agreed with the director and his review of the standoff and subsequent assault on the property. Hubbard gave additional details of the actual assault as he was one of the initial entry team members of the TACT Squad. Hubbard and fellow team member H. C. Ray forced entry through the rear doorway utilizing a battering ram. Hubbard and Ray then followed the rest of the team into the house, which had been prepped prior to the assault with thirty-six rounds of tear gas and flash bang concussion grenades. Their vision was severely hampered due to all the smoke, and Hubbard says that the assault team took fire almost instantly from a number of different locations. He stated that the team fired when they witnessed movement because they had drawn fire almost immediately upon entering the house. This gave them the impression that all the occupants were armed and because they had consistently refused all attempts to get them to surrender. Hubbard is quoted as saying, "When we spotted a figure, we tried to see who it was. When we determined it was not (Patrolman Robert S.) Hester, we fired. I was taking it for granted that they were armed." Keep in mind: this all was taking place in mere seconds. One reporter questioned him as to whether or not they would have accepted the surrender of any of the cultists to which he replied, "Sure, if we could have identified the person and had seen his hands up. But the situation was we had entered and drawn fire. We didn't know how many weapons were inside. When we saw movement, we fired. I never heard a sound out of any of them." He also stated that when an assault command is given, particularly in a hostage situation, police efforts shift from trying to negotiate surrender to trying to end the confrontation. He stated, "If it comes down to the assault that all negotiations have broken down, and in a situation like this one, that all parties are armed."

The commander of the TACT Squad, Captain Jim Music, released a statement shortly after the director's press conference. He stated:

> The Mission on Shannon wasn't a success. We lost lives. I can't help but think our record is a little tarnished, in that we did have to take lives. But then it was necessary, I don't feel a bit guilty about it, not one bit. I don't feel that any of my men feel that way. We are desperately to maintain the respect of our peers, our community and any element that would attempt to challenge us. We want their respect. We are very good at what we do, but we only do what we have to do.

> Anyone that starts a war, large or small, can expect to take casualties. Most police officers are a close knit group. Loyalty to each other is practically fanatical. An officer down call or an officer needs assistance call will bring them to the scene as swift as a hive of angry, disturbed hornets. I read where police officers have no code blue. Don't bet your life on it. They have a no nothing see nothing or hear nothing code concerning each other . . . that insulates them against the outside world.

Meanwhile, the department had other issues to deal with. For example, what about the men who were involved in the initial assault on the officers, but left before help arrived? The department knew the identity of these men. They were the following: Tyrone Henley, 27; James Murphy, Jr., 29; Thomas Carter Smith, 28; Reginald McCray, 29; Jackie Robinson Young, 25; Fred Lee Davis, 28; Joe E. Coleman, Jr., 29.

The men who stayed inside and subsequently died along with Lindberg Sanders were Larnell Sanders, 27 (Lindberg Sanders's son); Michael Delane Coleman, 18; David Lee Jordan, 30; Andrew Houston, 19; Cassell Harris, 21; and Earl Thomas, 20.

One man who was charged of the seven was Tyrone Henley. Patrolman Ray Schwill was called to testify at a preliminary hearing for Henley. He testified that the incident began when he and Patrolman Robert Hester were attacked by a group of approximately fifteen men. During the hearing in General Sessions Court, Schwill related the events of that fateful day. "There were maybe five or six people on me, I saw my partner (Officer Hester) briefly, maybe twice, and he was covered in people." At the conclusion of the hearing, Judge Ann Pugh ordered Henley be bound over to the grand jury on a charge of assault with intent to kill. The judge denied a request from Henley's attorney, Kenny Armstrong, that the charge be dismissed because Schwill could not positively indentify Henley's specific actions during the attack. The judge also refused the defense request to have bail lowered from $250,000 to $100,000.

Another of the men who escaped after hostilities began was arrested. T. C. Smith was taken into custody not long afterward. Smith was charged with three counts of aggravated assault. When he was arrested, the department reported that the arrest was a "breakthrough in the investigation" and that Henley had made some initial statements that assisted in the investigation. Henley was there and as such offered much detail into the circumstances that had taken place. No one who remained in the building after the initial kidnapping of the officers remained alive. Henley's information proved invaluable to the police.

Henley eventually admitted to striking Officer Schwill in the head. He stated, "I hit Officer Schwill with my fist upside the head or somewhere, and the next thing I know, I had got pushed back by the crowd." Henley eventually pleaded guilty on July 1, 1983, to attempting to commit a felony in the episode and was sentenced to a year in the Shelby County Correctional Center.

Smith was assigned a young, aggressive public defender, A. C. Wharton. Within a short period of time, Wharton was able to get all charges against Smith dropped. Of the seven men who were in the house at the time the assault on the officers occurred, only two were ever charged with a crime, and none ever spent time in jail for what they had done. The impression at the time as related by many was that the city simply wanted to see the incident disappear. Everyone seemed to be exhausted by the events that had taken place. The city had been tarnished by these events, and no one was looking forward to the matter being dragged through the criminal justice system again.

Meanwhile, it was time for the investigation to begin in earnest. The public had been shocked by what had happened, and they wanted answers. Some in the local black community and certain members of the NAACP were screaming that the police had murdered Sanders and his followers. They claimed that they had all been lined up against a wall inside the house and systematically killed, one by one. Tensions were running high at this point in the city. The police director and the mayor promised a complete, unbiased investigation into the incident. Many clamored for a federal investigation.

According to the report released by the coroner's office in Memphis, led by the coroner, Dr. Jerry Francisco, also the lead investigator, the men inside suffered the following wounds:

Larnell Sanders: 1-.223 round to the head, entering on the left and travelling to the right, also 1-.223 round to the left side of the chest, right to left.

Michael Coleman: 1-.223 round to the right arm, 1-.223 round right palm to wrist to the head. 1-.223 round to the right wrist and forearm.

David Jordan: 1-12 gauge shotgun blast to the head and 1-.223 round left to right in left arm.

Cassell Harris: 1-.223 shot to rear of head, left to right.

Earl Thomas: 1-.223 graze, front to rear. Hit right arm and chest. 1-.223 round left front abdomen, 1-.223 left forearm into chest, and 1-.223 round face.

Lindberg Sanders: 1-.38 to left wrist, 1-.223 round graze right temple, 1-.223 round top head, front to rear, up and down.

Andrew Houston: 3-.223 to face. 1-.38 in the back and possible .38 in the hand.

The autopsy report on Officer Hester was eventually released. He suffered numerous injuries all over his body. He had stab wounds, burns, contusions, lacerations, and much more. It was obvious that he had been severely beaten and tortured over an extended period of time before he finally died. A police department flashlight was found inside the house, and the medical examiner determined that this was the primary weapon used to murder Officer Hester. He had been struck some eighteen times about the head and face with this weapon. A rumor had circulated throughout the ranks of the department that Hester had been castrated. It was only one of countless rumors flowing throughout the city. This one proved to be false.

Some questions lingered after the dust had settled on Shannon Street. People were confused, and many were angry for a myriad of different reasons. For example, the raid was carried out after it was believed that Hester was already dead. Why wait until after the hostage dies to finally attempt an assault? If the prevailing thought was he was already dead, why not simply starve out Sanders and his group? Simply wear them down and hope that they surrender peacefully. In retrospect, it is easy to second-guess the decisions made in the heat of the moment. Holt and the rest of his advisors on the scene believed that if they went in earlier, Hester would have been murdered by Lindberg Sanders as many thought he was standing over him with a loaded and cocked pistol pointed at his head. He repeatedly threatened to blow his head off if anyone attempted to enter the structure. There is no way that Sanders could have been standing over Hester for thirty hours without moving in order to carry out this threat. The department had no way to know when he was near Hester and when he had moved away. Nor did they know if perhaps another member might have been watching over him, ready to kill him as soon as he detected the beginnings of an assault. Director Holt, to his credit, took full responsibility for the decision to first delay, then to assault the house. He stood behind his decision by stating, "I was backed up by the unanimous opinion of probably 250 years of police experience." He assumed that the hostage takers would quickly realize that they had no chance to escape and the negotiations would eventually win out. Sadly, this was not the case.

The second-guessing continued. Sanders's wife often wondered what would have happened if she had been permitted to speak to her husband. Officers on the scene wondered why the decision to storm the house was made after Hester died. It is inevitable that people who were there would wonder what would have happened if things had been handled differently. We'll never know for certain. What happened was a tragedy for the victims, but also a tragedy for the citizens of Memphis. This incident helped to further along the racism that continues to invade politics in this city to this very day. There is not a person who was there that was not touched in some profound way. Some suffered from post-traumatic stress syndrome. Some suffered in silence. Some turned to drink. Marriages crumbled and the strain was almost for the city to cope with. All were affected.

The United States Justice Department conducted an investigation into the Shannon Street siege. The investigation lasted for well over a year. The investigators combed over every piece of evidence available. Shortly after the bodies were removed, the police department ordered a complete lockdown of the premises. A team of officers with video recorders entered and methodically swept and recorded each room. Photographers were on the scene taking pictures before the bodies were removed. Each and every frame and photograph was thoroughly examined for evidence of any wrongdoing by the assault teams. The justice department concluded that there were "no prosecutable violations of federal civil rights or criminal laws" in the incident that left eight people dead. Justice Department Spokesman John Wilson described the investigation as "comprehensive" and said it included interviews with both participants and witnesses, along with analysis of the physical and medical evidence. Physical evidence was gathered and evaluated by a team of agents from the FBI laboratory in Washington, Wilson said, while an independent analysis of the medical evidence was conducted by forensic specialists from the Walter Reed Army Medical Center. The FBI investigation, which the justice department relied upon in part in coming to the conclusion of no wrongdoing both civilly and criminally, included interviews with police officers, neighbors, family members, and anyone else even remotely involved with the case. The wording of the statement was strange, to say the least. Many in the black community in Memphis and elsewhere believed that the police had gotten away with murder. The statement certainly gave room for doubt. It was clear and at the same time unclear to virtually everybody.

US Attorney Hickman Ewing of Memphis concurred with the decision. He was the first to formally request an investigation from the justice department.

He and his staff had also conducted their own investigation and had arrived at the same conclusion as the one rendered in Washington. Ewing was quoted as saying after the justice department's ruling, "If I had disagreed with it, I would be objecting to it. We're not taking one side or the other, but based on the evidence available I do not disagree with it." Once again, a clear statement on the part of the US attorney, but it still left room for doubt, primarily because of the way in which it was worded.

However, Maxine Smith, the executive secretary of the local chapter of the NAACP, was infuriated with the decision. She stated that "a great injustice had been rendered." She also said, "This is shocking. As we look at the racism that pervades this country and particularly this administration, we should not be surprised. But we can't help but be very disappointed that the administration of justice and our top lawmaking officials have no concern for the rights and protection of black citizens." Ms. Smith was not inside the house that night and had no way to know everything that took place, but she was convinced that racism played a part in the deaths of the inhabitants of the dwelling. Many were disgusted by her actions. Most of them sought an investigation by outsiders. If they determined that there were additional crimes committed, then prosecutions should take place. But should the investigation conclude that no crimes were committed, then the matter should be dropped so that the healing could continue. However, she obviously felt the need to further inflame the passions of the people of Memphis, both black and white. Ms. Smith conducted no investigation of her own. She had no evidence to support her claim whatsoever. She merely concluded that because the offenders were black and the murdered officer was white, then the assault team must have gone in with the express purpose to murder everyone inside, simply because of the color of their skin.

Some family members hired attorneys in order to file a lawsuit against the police department and the city. The first suit was filed almost one year to the day after the incident began. One of these, local attorney John Schaeffer Jr. commented after the Justice Department ruling, that it would have no impact on the upcoming civil proceedings. He eventually filed lawsuits demanding 17.5 million dollars against the city and police department. John Schaeffer and his son, John Schaeffer Jr., stated in the suit that the shootings by the police were "unwarranted, cruel, inhuman, unjustifiable, and involved the excessive use of force under the circumstances." Schaeffer also commented that the incident was a "gross use of excessive force by the police department." He further went on to say that Sanders and the others were "found guilty and executed on the scene" for the death of Officer Hester. He claimed that officers knew before the shootings that Sanders was mentally ill but refused any offer of help from Sanders's physician. This suit was followed quickly by another suit filed by Attorney Herman Morris (who would, years later, run unsuccessfully for mayor of Memphis) on behalf of the wives of Sanders and Sanders's son, Larnell. The suits were filed against

Mayor Dick Hackett, Police Director John Holt, TACT Squad Commander Jim Music, Patrolman Ray Schwill, and TACT Squad members R. O. Watson, C. R. Summers, Don Rutherford, Kenny McNair, Dave Hubbard, and H. A. Ray and Patrolman W. R. Aiken. The mayor refused to comment on the allegations contained in the suit.

One of the issues confronting the attorneys was the city's refusal to release any documents pertaining to the incident. The local newspaper filed a lawsuit under the Freedom of Information Act in order to force the city to make public all the records. The city fought against releasing the documents, but eventually, the courts ruled that they had to comply with the requests for information. The city appealed the decision all the way to the Tennessee Supreme Court, which ruled against the city on May 12, 1986. However, as the case dragged through the courts for years, the stalling tactics employed by the city helped to fuel speculation that the city was trying to hide something. Eventually, the newspaper won out, and the Memphis Police Department was ordered to release all documents pertaining to the Shannon Street incident. This was a small victory for those in the community and elsewhere who wanted the unvarnished truth. The lawyers representing the families suing the city and key officers involved in the Shannon Street assault were happy to be able to secure access to the volumes and volumes of police reports filed after the incident happened. They had suffered a blow when the report of the federal investigation was released that exonerated the department and its officers from any wrongdoing. Now they have unrestricted access to the police files they hoped would turn up a smoking gun that would prove the officers acted criminally in their assault of the house on Shannon Street. The attorneys and their assistants spent hundreds of hours looking for any document that might show ulterior motives behind the police department's handling of the situation. They were never able to come up with anything substantial to bolster their case against the city, and eventually, both cases were dismissed. The lawyers representing the families had lost. Nothing further would be done, and finally, the city could begin the healing process.

As time passed, occasionally the news media would report new stories about the Shannon Street incident. In 1990, an alleged witness, who lived behind the house at 2239 Shannon Street, claimed that he witnessed three subjects raise their hands and exit the rear door of the house. He said he saw police officers intercept the three subjects and force them back into the house. He went on to state that shortly thereafter he heard shots coming from inside the house, giving him the impression that the officers had taken the three subjects back inside the house and executed them. This made news for a couple of days in Memphis and then, as the story was preposterous to begin with, the media abandoned it. On the twenty-fifth anniversary of the incident, one local attorney got before the cameras and claimed that he had new evidence proving wrongdoing on the part of the police department, but nothing ever came of it. He got a few minutes of television time and then was promptly forgotten, until the next incident involving race came up.

The city in 2010 remains much the same as it did in 1983. Certainly, things have improved dramatically in many ways. The racial divide is as not as intense today as it was in 1983, but it remains to some degree. The city in now estimated to be 70 percent black and has had a black mayor for almost the past twenty years. The majority of the city council is black as opposed to 1983 when the numbers were reversed. Then the mayor was white and the city council predominantly white. So while the racial makeup of the city has changed over the years, the problems persist. Racism still dominates the headlines far too often. Some politicians seem to want it that way in this city. Most are progressive and seek only the best interests of their constituents. However, there remain a few who seem to see racism around every corner.

The Shannon Street incident was a tragedy for all involved. The ramifications of it still permeate the area to this day. Most local people nowadays have a vague recollection of the incident, and most people under the age of thirty have no idea what Shannon Street was.

The police department still teaches in the academy the handling of the situation. Officer Russ Aiken has become a legend to all police officers, both black and white. His performance that night is still taught as being perhaps one of the finest performances in the history of law enforcement.

In the end, the best we can hope for is that we have learned the lessons of Shannon Street so that something like this can never happen again.

EPILOGUE

The years have passed, and most people involved want nothing more than to put this incident behind them and move forward. The pain generated that night has lasted a long time. To this day, in my interviews with the participants, all suffer some sort of traumatic stress-related problems even after more than twenty-five years. Some are unable or unwilling to relive the memories of that evening. Patrolman Ray Schwill refused to be interviewed for this project. He told me that it was still too painful to talk about and that he felt that he had not been treated fairly by the press in the past. It made this project more difficult, but Officer Schwill has absolutely nothing to feel guilty about. He was simply a man doing his job when he entered that house. I do believe that no matter which two officers who responded to that call, they would have met a similar fate. Schwill and Hester just happened to be in the wrong place at the wrong time. Both were trained to gain control of the environment and to not lose it. Gain the upper hand and keep it. That's exactly what they tried to do, and it led to tragic consequences that were far beyond their control. No one could have predicted the events that took place. They did everything exactly as they had been trained to, and still, it was not enough.

The police director, John Holt, took the bulk of the heat for what ended up happening. He took pressure from not only the public at large and the media, but also from the officers he was charged with leading. The universal thought among the rank and file at the time was that Holt was responsible for the death of one of their own due to his refusal to attempt a rescue while Hester was still alive. Holt weathered both storms and went on to a distinguished career with the police department. The Memphis Police Academy today is named in his honor. Ray Maples, the president of the police officers' union at the time and one of the most vocal critics of how the department handled the events on Shannon Street, interestingly now supports the actions of Director Holt. Maples was quoted the next day blasting the command staff, but later retracted his criticisms claiming that he misspoke in the heat of the moment. On the twenty-fifth anniversary of the event, Maples was back on television refuting the charges from a local activist about racism. His now frail stature still holds the passion he maintains over Shannon Street.

It is easy for the reader to second-guess the decisions made that night. Monday-morning quarterbacking is inevitable. Holt believed that Lindberg Sanders was holding a gun to the head of Officer Hester and that any attempt to rescue him would have resulted in disaster. He firmly thought that negotiation was the best way to resolve this situation peaceably. Normally, in any hostage situation, the course of action is to begin negotiations immediately and attempt to wear down the hostage takers. They will listen to the demands the subjects make and then work from there. Time usually always favors the negotiators. Holt and the mayor had no idea that it was going to end up the way it did. In all his years in law enforcement, he had never come across a situation like this one. Sanders made no rational demands; in fact, the only demand he made in thirty hours of attempts was his request to speak to the disc jockey. Hostage situations usually always ended after lengthy negotiations and everyone had walked away without injury. Wearing down the hostage taker works in the vast majority of occurrences.

There was a lot of talk at the time that Lindberg Sanders was the leader of some sort of local cult. While it certainly had some characteristics normally associated with cultlike activity, I doubt that today it would be defined as such. The tragic events in Guyana were still fresh in the minds of many people so defining the group as cultists was inevitable. His odd behavior would lead one to believe that a cult was what he led. Remember the times, and it will help to explain the media's infatuation with cults. Lindberg Sanders was simply the head of a loosely organized group of men who met occasionally at his home to party and listen to the entertaining ramblings of the leader of the group said as gospel. There were those who would follow him wherever he would lead, and it led to their tragic early deaths.

In spending an enormous amount of time researching this story, I came to the conclusion that there were no intentional criminal acts on the part of law enforcement. It would have been impossible to keep any conspiracy to murder Sanders and his followers a secret. Someone would have objected and gone public with this information. To assume that all the members of the Memphis Police Department on the scene over those thirty hours would have kept quiet after all these years is quite a stretch. The media had been present for most of the time, and if there was any kind of conspiracy planned, they most certainly would have gotten wind of it. Mistakes were clearly made. Communications between the officers on the scene and between the command staff headquartered in the elementary school directly across the street certainly should have been better than they were. One hand did not seem to know what the other hand was doing. Officers were tired and it was very cold. There was intense pressure on the staff from many different sides. Judgment calls were made throughout the thirty hours. Some were correct, but too many were not. You could say that fate played a hand that night but that would be to oversimplify things.

When conducting interviews for this book, I was often asked my opinion as to why it turned out the way that it did. I have given a lot of thought to that question over the past year. Initially, I placed the blame for the failure of the police department to end the situation peacefully right on the shoulder of the mayor at the time. After all, was not he the one that ultimately had to approve the actions taken by the police department? I also held the police director responsible. After all, he was the leader supposedly making the decisions at the time. And as events unfolded, many of his decisions would turn out wrong.

He had little intelligence to work with and couple that with a psychotic, unstable individual working against him, things were bound to go wrong somewhere. But ultimately, I have come to the conclusion that no one person is responsible completely. It was a very horrific scenario that no one could have predicted. And Holt had no experience in dealing with psychotic hostage takers. No one did back in those days. He simply did the best he could have done under the circumstances. And the mayor was ill equipped to handle something like this. He relied upon his instinct and the advice of his advisors, including key members of the police department.

But ultimately, I place the blame on the part of Lindberg Sanders and his followers. They had thirty hours in which to surrender to authorities. They did not have to murder Officer Hester. They could have given up at any time and walked away with relatively minor charges. But they didn't. They elected to beat the officer continuously until his eventual death. If Sanders was in control of his followers, and it appears that he had quite a bit of control over them, then he could have ended things at any time. Sanders's followers could also have surrendered at any time during the thirty hours. They were all grown men with their own minds. At least six of them realized things were going to get ugly, so they fled from the house shortly after Hester was taken hostage. Anyone of the remaining suspects could have simply walked out one of the doors and given themselves up. But Sanders had convinced most of the group that the end of the world was coming and that this was it. Two of his followers told their wives shortly beforehand that they most likely would not be returning. Sanders himself told his wife, when she was going to the cleaners, not to worry about it for reasons that are now all too obvious, but at the time it was merely Lindberg acting strangely as he often did when he was not taking his medications. Cultlike? Most certainly. The police department often referred to Sanders and his followers as being members of a cult. The media played up this angle at every opportunity. Any mention of the word *cult* piqued the interest of most people. It sold a lot of newspapers and sounded good as a lead-in to local newscasts. In the days before every event from bake sales to mass murders on television became breaking news, mention the word *cult* and media people knew they would have a captive audience.

I feel that Sanders and his group of followers wanted to die that night in order to fulfill his prophecy. It ended up being a situation now referred to as suicide by cop. But I do not believe that it was as simple as suicide by cop. In suicide-by-cop scenarios, the offender usually does not want to harm anyone except himself. Sanders clearly wanted people to die. Back then, this term did not exist. Now it is an all too common occurrence that is studied at length by professionals. All police officers now are trained to recognize the characteristics of this all-too-common occurrence.

Other aspects of this case continue to baffle many people. For example, during the siege, many different officers reported hearing sounds of construction taking place inside the house. Officers feared that barricades were being constructed to make their eventual entry more difficult. Yet when the dust settled, no reference was ever made to any new construction inside the house. What were they doing? Why were sounds of hammering being heard and for what purpose? I suppose we'll never know. When the investigation began, why weren't the walls inside the house taken down and searched? Were the men inside trying to hide something which might explain the sounds of construction? Not one of the officers I spoke to remembers the walls of the house being torn down to search for additional weapons or contraband.

A number of different people had informed officers on the scene that Sanders and his followers were avid hunters and that many different weapons were in the house. And yet after the house was searched, the only weapons found were the two revolvers from the officers. However, in one of the crime scene photographs, a telescopic sight from a rifle is clearly present on a coffee table in the living room. Its presence was never explained by anyone.

When dealing with irrational subjects, it is impossible to use conventional rational thinking to determine why things happen the way they do. The mysteries that surround Shannon Street many never be revealed. The only people who know what actually took place that fateful cold January day took that information with them to the grave. Had Lindberg Sanders been taking his medications, then one has to believe that this entire incident would have never happened. Eight people would have lived a long time. Their families would have been able to enjoy their company and guidance. They would probably have raised children and would now be looking forward to retiring. Because one man decided, for whatever reasons, not to continue taking his prescribed medication, dozens of people were robbed of the opportunity to enjoy and relish in the company of now long dead family members. A selfish act committed by a selfish man. If he so clearly wanted to see the end of the world, what motivated him to take so many others with him?

No one could have ever predicted an occurrence of this nature ever occurring. We can only hope and pray it never does again.

WHERE ARE THEY NOW?

Ed Vidulich

Patrolman Vidulich stood behind the large oak tree in the front yard at Shannon Street for hours underneath the hand-painted sign nailed to the tree referring to "Death to Mr. Hog." He was close enough to the entrance to spit and hit it, but was powerless to change the events of that night. Vidulich remained on the Memphis Police Department, eventually reaching the rank of lieutenant. His last assignment was to head up the Mississippi River contingency of the MPD. He was in the process of combining two households when he befriended a local young man. He took him under his wing and became what he many perceived to be a mentor of some kind to him. Tragically, the young man turned out to be nothing more than a local thug, and he ended up murdering Lieutenant Vidulich in the kitchen of his home. The Memphis Police Department lost one of the finest people to ever serve the citizens of the city. By all account, Ed Vidilich was a class act and well loved and respected by all. He is missed by all who ever knew or came in contact with him.

Tommy Turner

Officer Tommy Turner was one of the first officers to respond to the call from help from Schwill and Hester. He attempted to get in the front door and was beaten over the head as he entered. Fortunately, when he was struck, he fell backward, out onto the porch, which most likely saved his life. Had he fallen into the house, he would have been taken hostage, and Sanders and his followers would have had another cop to beat and torture and another weapon at their disposal. Turner remained with the Memphis Police Department and served with distinction until his retirement in the spring of 2009. Turner had been elected president of the Memphis Police Officers Association and served until his reelection bid failed. The election was bitterly contested and extremely hostile in many ways. Turner lost the election to one of his bitter foes, and after they took office, they claimed that record keeping done by Turner and his staff was lacking in professionalism. They promptly began a series of audits into the finances of the association. As of this writing, nothing concrete has been revealed. Turner served decades with the department, and his reputation was excellent. The people of the city of Memphis were well protected when Tommy Turner was on the job.

A. C. Wharton

A. C. Wharton was the young public defender assigned to defend one of the two men charged in the Shannon Street murder of Officer Hester. He was able to get the charges against his client dropped, and Wharton remained with the public defender's office earning a reputation as a tough but fair negotiator. Wharton rode his success within the public defender's office to the mayors' office in Shelby County. He was a good public defender and oftentimes a voice of reason and calm in the racially polarized city of Memphis. He was recently elected by the citizens of the city of Memphis as mayor.

Ray Schwill

Officer Schwill eventually survived his physical wounds. Only he can describe the psychological wounds and how successful he has been in dealing with it. Any guilt he may have endured from the way events transpired is purely in his own mind. Nothing he could have done would have altered the outcome. He and Hester entered a scene neither one had ever encountered before; indeed, no officer ever had to face what they were up against. He was simply a cop who was thrust into a situation no one had ever had to contend with. He and his partner were quickly ambushed and overwhelmed in the confined space of a tiny ranch home in North Memphis. Schwill's actions that night were instinctive. He and his partner had been jumped by numerous individuals and were unable to defend themselves. It was simply a twist of fate that allowed Schwill to escape while his partner could not. It could have just as easily been Schwill who was dragged into that side room. That room had only one entry in and out, and whoever was held captive inside would have been trapped. Officer Schwill eventually returned to the department. He had to endure the stares and sideway looks his fellow officers were certain to give him as he worked alongside of them. It would be inevitable that some few members of the department might blame him personally for Hester's death. This was absurd, and he knew it. He held his head high and dealt with all the issues. He knew he had done all that he could to save his partner. Self-doubt is not a characteristic that many good police officers possess. They have to be tough to survive the rigors of police work in a large city. Schwill's career with the MPD was exemplary. He steadily rose through the ranks until he reached one of the highest positions in the department. He retired after serving the citizens of Memphis for decades. He retired and eventually accepted a job running a local security company. He survived Shannon Street and moved on with his life although I have no doubt that Shannon Street is never far from his thoughts.

Jim Kellum

Jim Kellum was the officer who successfully placed the microphone inside the house early in the morning. His actions allowed the officers in command to gain inside information into what was taking place inside the home. He approached the reporter from Atlanta and asked if he could borrow a microphone. He risked his life to attempt to rescue Officer Hester. He negotiated the narrow path between the two houses to place the microphone inside a broken windowpane. As he approached the window, if he had been spotted by anyone inside, he would have been a sitting duck. There was nowhere for him to run. The space between the two brick houses was less than six feet. It was a tremendous act of courage to risk everything to get that microphone inside. It seemed as though whenever there was action around anywhere, Kellum was there. He had a unique ability to take risks that very few would ever attempt and succeed in getting the job done.

Kellum had a long and fruitful career with the Memphis Police Department. His courage and dedication to the people and the department was unparalleled in the history of the MPD. He was later to win one of the department's highest awards for bravery where he, once again, placed his life on the line in order to save another. He knew the dangers inherent with the job. While others might hide from their sworn duty, Jim Kellum could always be counted on to get the job done.

Kellum retired and built him and his lovely wife a dream home on a quiet river in Mississippi. His "man cave" affords Kellum the quiet solitude he deserves. As you go through the house, you would be hard-pressed to determine what this man did for a living. That is until you notice a small display hanging on a wall near his large-screen television set. That's where the Medal of Honor sits behind an unimposing glass display. Jim's health has been failing in recent years, and he has recently bounced back from a minor stroke. He runs a successful security business from his home, and as long as his health remains good, Jim will continue to succeed in anything he chooses to do.

Russ Aiken

Officer Aiken was awarded the second highest award for bravery by the Memphis Police Department for his actions in early January 1983. His repeated attempts to save his brother officers that night are the stuff of heroes. Hollywood could not have planned a more imposing man. He can take credit for saving the life of Officer Schwill as his repeated assaults, all alone, into the back door to rescue the hostages led to the suspects abandoning Officer Schwill to confront the new threat Aiken posed. As Schwill pretended to be dead, the suspects felt they could leave him alone as they rushed to deal with Aiken's repeated attacks. Had they simply checked Schwill's pulse, they would have known in an instant that he was still very much alive. Aiken never gave them the chance. As the suspects rushed to the rear of the house, this gave Schwill the opportunity to rush out the front door. Horribly wounded in the head and hand, it's doubtful he would ever have been able to escape without the diversion Aiken provided. If ever there were a war and I could pick any man in the world to have next to me in a foxhole, that man would be Russ Aiken.

As with most of the officers involved in the Shannon Street incident, Russ Aiken remained a valuable member of the Memphis Police Department for decades. He served as vice president of the Memphis Patrolman's Association for a number of years. The president of the association during Aiken's tenure was Tommy Turner, who was also at Shannon Street and was injured as he and Aiken attempted to enter the house (Turner in the front door and Aiken in the rear). He finally retired in 2008 and began living his dream. He had always talked about a house in the mountains away from city life. He built a magnificent home on the side of a hill in Arkansas. He and his family live a truly wonderful life. Their children reflect the parents in the finest sense of the word. As I interviewed Russ, I was given the privilege of meeting his youngest son. He had joined the armed forces of the United States and was due to leave for boot camp in a few days. As they say, the apple doesn't fall far from the tree.

Ray Maples

Ray Maples was the president of the patrolman's union for the Memphis Police Department for many years. Although he had no official capacity at the scene on Shannon Street, Maples remained on the scene during the entire time. He approached the commanders on numerous times in order to try and convince them to begin the rescue attempts. Other officers there were looking to Maples to do something. As the head of the union, he was the natural selection to carry the torch for the patrolmen on the scene. Every time Maples attempted to reason with the command staff, he was rebuffed and told that they had the situation in hand. Essentially, "don't call us, we'll call you" is the attitude he encountered whenever he attempted to get something done. This happened a number of times until, as Maples tells it, he forced their hand by telling them that if they did not affect a rescue attempt immediately, then he would gather a group of willing police officers (of which there were many) and they would rescue Officer Hester. Fortunately, Maples never had to take this drastic action. Shortly after his final plea, the rescue attempt began. Did Maples's action have an impact on the decision to begin the rescue attempt? He certainly feels that it did, and he is probably correct. Either way, Maples's action that evening displayed to the troops that he was there for them and that his only concern was getting all his people out safe and sound.

On the twenty-fifth anniversary of the Shannon Street incident, Maples was interviewed on one of the local television newscasts. Maples appeared in his home, and you could see the pain etched on his face even after twenty-five years. He made the claim on the air about his actions that evening where he threatened to take action himself. It was the first time he had ever revealed this to anyone. Maples retired after serving over twenty years with the Memphis Police Department. He feels that he retired too soon and regrets not staying in for his thirty years. Memphis had a policy at the time whereby officers who remained on the job for thirty years were automatically promoted to the rank of captain. They could then retire at that rank and garner a higher retirement package. Maples missed out on this program by only a few years, but he felt that at the time he was ready to begin a new career. The dual frustrations of being a cop coupled with the additional responsibilities of being a union president had worn him down to the point where he couldn't deal with it any longer. It was time to move on.

Maples worked on a number of capacities since his retirement. Nothing gave him the satisfaction that police work did. At least, not until recently. Ray Maples has gone back to school. He is studying to become a preacher. He has found a renewed commitment in his life. Regrettably, fate has dealt Maples a devastating blow. He has been diagnosed with a life-threatening illness, and he has been in the fight of his life. We're all praying for his recovery, and if anyone can beat this, it's Ray Maples.

Dorothy Sanders

The wife of Lindberg Sanders and mother of Larnell lives peacefully in a home in the North Memphis area known as Frayser. She suffered quietly for many years and eventually became a home health care nurse. She has loved ones who live nearby and are constantly with her. She and her entire family maintain to this day that the shootings were completely unnecessary. She steadfastly maintains the killings of the Shannon Street Seven were a direct result of the police wanting someone to pay for what happened to Officers Hester and Schwill. In other words, the Memphis Police Department acted simply for revenge. Many people in the black community felt the same way. Some also believed that it was inevitable that, after the murder of Officer Hester, the fate of Lindberg Sanders and his follower was sealed.

She battled bouts of depression over the years and ended up adopting two special needs children. All her children remain close to her, and she sees them frequently. They recognize the failings of Lindberg Sanders but choose to remember only the good times. Dorothy remained single all these years and devoted her life to the needs of others. She is a classy lady and deserves to live out her remaining days in peace. One has to wonder what would have been had Lindberg Sanders taken his medications. The love of a good woman and wonderful mother was not enough for Lindberg Sanders. No doubt, many lives would have been saved.

If there is a lesson to be learned in all this, it is that police officers responding to normally routine calls should always be on the alert for unknown issues. Having been on many different police calls over the years, I can say with a degree of certainty that this is easier said than done. Police officers do not enjoy the most exciting job in the world, most of the time anyway. I once had a Chicago Police Department sergeant tell me right after I started that police work is defined by 99 percent sheer boredom and 1 percent adrenaline rush that would be impossible to ever duplicate.

Many officers rely upon a sixth sense to help identify potential problems. Usually, this can work, but sometimes it does not and that's when you can get into serious trouble. Better to heed the warnings of the old police sergeant in the vintage television series *Hill Street Blues* who used to end every roll call with the words, "Let's be careful out there."

INDEX

A

Abdul, Minster, 109
Aiken, Russ, 57, 131, 142

B

Bowman, Paul, 72-74

C

Carr, M., 50
Clark, Dave, 44
Coleman, Joe, Jr., 125
Coleman, Michael Delane, 31-32, 125, 127
coroner's report, 127
Cottingham, Joe, 44
Cox, Jean, 72
Crawford, James, 44
Creasy, Charlotte, 14
Cummins, Jo, 72

D

Davis, Fred Lee, 125
Davy Crockett, 18
Downen, William, 69

E

Ed Vidulich, 48, 59, 69-70, 81, 139
Ewing, Hickman, 128

F

Forrest, Nathan Bedford, 19
Francisco, Jerry, 127

G

Goulet, Jean Claude, 71

H

Hackett, Dick, 79, 88, 130
Harris, Cassell, 32-33, 127
Henley, Tyrone, 125-26

Hester, Robert
  arriving at Sanders's house, 38–39
  autopsy report on, 127
  being beaten, 80–81
  involvement in Kansas Street incident,
    44–45
  life story of, 45–46
  professional profile of, 42–43
  rescuing, 96–104
  taken hostage, 47
Holt, John, 78–79, 133
  press conference with, 113–24
  press statement of, 109–20
  professional profile of, 76–77
Hoover, J. Edgar, 21
Houston, Andrew, 33, 125, 127
Hubbard, Dave, 94, 124, 130

I

identity theft, 25

J

James, Bob, 113
Jordan, David Lee, 125

K

Kellum, Jim, 73, 82–83, 91, 141
Kelly, George, 21
King, Martin Luther, Jr., 21
Knight, Joe, 20

M

Maples, Ray, 89–90, 104, 142–43
Marten, George, 72
McCray, Reginald, 125
McNair, K. K., 96
Memphis Police Academy, 21, 133
Memphis Police Department

differences between dispatchers and
    officers, 35–37
  duties and pay of officers in, 17–18
  first pursuit vehicle of, 20
  history of, 18–22
  hostage taking in St. Jude's, 71–72
  identifies the men behind the assault,
    125
  lawsuits filed against, 129–30
  periodic vehicle testing, 21
  probationary officers in, 42
  purse-snatching call for the, 16
  rescuing hostages in St. Jude's, 73–74
  thin blue line of, 85–86
Mhoon, V. J., 23
Michael Coleman, 31, 39, 127
Murphy, James, Jr., 32, 125
Music, Jim, 125–26

N

NAACP (National Association for the
    Advancement of Colored People),
    113, 126
Norton, James, 58–60

O

Onion Field, The (Wambaugh), 76

P

Parker, Steve, 57
Perry, Oliver Hazard, 20
post-traumatic stress disorder, 133
Public, John Q., 50

R

racism, 128–29, 131
Ray, H. C., 98, 124
Renfrow, K., 23

Ross, Don, 23
Rutherford, Don, 94, 98, 130

S

Sanders, Dorothy, 32-33, 143
Sanders, Larnell, 125, 127
Sanders, Lindberg
  assault preparations for, 93-95
  beliefs taught by, 26-27
  ending hostage assault, 109
  fighting against police officers, 35-37
  house construction of, 29, 87
  mental deterioration of, 29-30, 32, 34,
    48, 81
  negotiations with, 75-77, 78-79
  profile of, 28-29
  strategies to catch, 82-84
Schaeffer, John, Jr., 129
Schwill, Ray, 11, 39-40, 48-49
  after the hostage, 140-41
  escape of, 51
  escape plan of, 48-49
  held hostage, 11
  testifying against Henley, Tyrone, 126
Smith, Maxine, 129
Smith, Thomas Carter, 32-33, 125-26
St. Jude Children's Hospital, 71-72
suicide by cop, 74, 136
Summers, C. R., 94, 100, 130
SWAT (Special Weapons and Tactics), 56
Sykes, John Wesley, Jr., 14

T

TACT (Tactical Ammunition Control), 95
Thomas, Danny, 72
Thomas, Earl, 125, 127
Thomas, Marlo, 72
traffic violations, pursuit for, 15
Turner, Tommy, 50-52, 102, 110, 139-40

U

United States Justice Department
    investigation, 128

V

Vidulich, Ed, 69-70, 139

W

Wambaugh, Joseph
  Onion Field, The, 76
Waters, Maxine, 109, 112
Watson, Lance, 109
Watson, R., 50
Wharton, A. C., 126, 140
Wilson, John, 128

Y

Young, Jackie Robinson, 125

Made in the USA
Lexington, KY
12 August 2015